PAPER WINGS

Pages from Little Dreamers

Budding Authors of

Vailankanni Public School - CBSE,

Krishnagiri.

Address: #21-D, TNHB, Phase 2, Rayakottai Road,
Krishnagiri - 635001, Krishnagiri District, Tamil Nadu

Website: vpscbsekrishnagiri.com | Phone: 9095-192-192

VPSKGI

Clever Fox® PUBLISHING

Chennai • Bangalore

CLEVER FOX PUBLISHING
Chennai, India

Published by CLEVER FOX PUBLISHING 2026

ISBN: 978-93-7500-025-9

CONTENTS

FROM THE CHAIRMAN

True education extends far beyond the four walls of a classroom. It is about empowering young minds to think critically, dream fearlessly, and articulate their vision of the world.

Paper Wings stands as a testament to this philosophy.

When we established **Vailankanni Public School – CBSE, Krishnagiri** our vision was to create an environment where academic excellence and creative brilliance walk hand in hand. Holding this book, written entirely by our students, I feel a profound sense of fulfillment. These pages prove that we are raising not just learners, but thinkers and creators who are ready to make their mark on the world.

To our young authors: Your words have power. Use them wisely, and never stop exploring the depths of your potential. I commend the editorial team and the staff for bringing this beautiful project to fruition.

Dr. M. Thambidurai, M.P.,
Founder & Chairman
Member of Parliament (Rajya Sabha)
Former Union Minister, New Delhi
Former Deputy Speaker of the Lok Sabha

FROM THE TRUSTEE

There is no greater satisfaction than seeing the seeds we plant today bloom into flowers of creativity and wisdom. As a Trustee of **Vailankanni Public School – CBSE, Krishnagiri** I have always believed that our role is to provide the soil and sunshine for our students to grow.

Paper Wings is the beautiful harvest of that effort.

Reading the contributions in this volume has been a delightful journey. From innocent observations to surprisingly profound insights, these children have reminded us of the purity and clarity with which they view the world. It is a privilege to support an institution that values these voices and gives them a platform to be heard.

I extend my warmest wishes to the students, parents, and faculty. May this publication encourage even more students to pick up their pens and let their imaginations soar.

Dr. M. Lasya Thambidurai,
MBBS, M.D., FRCR (London)
Trustee

FROM THE CORRESPONDENT

It is often said that every child is an artist, and the problem is how to remain an artist once we grow up.

As I turn the pages of **Paper Wings,** I am reminded that our primary duty as educators is not just to fill minds with facts, but to keep that artistic spark alive.

This book is not merely a collection of stories and poems; it is a window into the unfiltered, vibrant, and boundless imaginations of our students at Vailankanni Public School. In an era dominated by screens and swift digital consumption, seeing our children pause, reflect, and express themselves through the written word is both heartening and vital.

I congratulate the young authors for their courage to share their thoughts, and the teachers who have so gently guided these budding talents. May this book be the first of many milestones in your creative journeys.

S. Kootharasan, MBA
Correspondent

PRINCIPAL'S PEN

It gives me immense joy and pride to present this book as a first-time effort by our young writers who have stepped into the world of storytelling with courage and creativity. This collection is not just a set of stories; it is a reflection of their imagination, curiosity, and willingness to try something new.

Each group and each individual child has contributed in their own unique way, bringing their thoughts to life through words. Their enthusiasm and originality have made this project truly special, and I deeply appreciate the hard work, guidance, and support that went into shaping it.

This milestone reminds us that when children are encouraged to explore and express themselves, they can achieve remarkable things. I look forward to many more such initiatives that nurture their talents and celebrate their voices.

Mrs. V. Vijayalakshmi
Principal
Vailankanni Public School – CBSE
Krishnagiri

PREFACE

This book is a collection of short stories created by young minds who have taken their first steps into the world of writing. Each child has chosen a topic close to their heart and expressed it in the way they see and understand the world. Their ideas may have been inspired by teachers, parents, friends, or other sources, but every story carries the child's own imagination, creativity, and effort.

Through this process, our young writers have not only explored their storytelling abilities but have also strengthened their language skills and confidence. We believe that such experiences encourage them to dream boldly and reach great heights in the future.

All the stories submitted have been included in this book. The content has been kept as close to the original as possible, with only minor edits made to ensure smooth reading while preserving the genuine voice of each child.

We hope this collection brings joy to our readers and inspires many more children to discover the writer within themselves.

ACKNOWLEDGMENTS

We express our sincere gratitude to the Almighty, whose blessings have made this book possible.

We thank the Management and our Principal for their continued support and for providing the opportunity to bring together these stories written by our young students.

Our heartfelt thanks to all the teachers for guiding and encouraging the children throughout this journey.

We extend our warm appreciation to the young writers, whose creativity, imagination, and unique voices have made this collection truly special.

We are grateful to the parents for their support and cooperation, which played a vital role in motivating the young writers.

We also acknowledge the dedicated efforts of the editorial team, including both technical and non-technical staff, for their hard work in preparing this book.

Finally, we extend our appreciation to everyone who contributed silently behind the scenes. Your efforts have helped bring this collection to life.

1

THE MOUNTAIN AND THE MOUSE

AADHIRA SREE S | GRADE 3

A small mouse was sitting at the foot of a great mountain. Seeing its tiny size, the mountain mocked, “I really pity you, a poor little creature, like you!”

The mouse calmly replied, "It's true that I'm small, but my size has its own advantages." The mountain boasted proudly, "Advantages? What can a small thing like you possibly do? Look at me! I can stop clouds and change their path across the sky."

The mouse nodded and said, "That's true. You are mighty indeed. But I too have my strengths. I can make several holes in your rocky base with ease. Now tell me, can you stop me from digging burrows in your body?" The mighty mountain fell silent, with nothing more to say.

2

BACKBONE OF OUR FUTURE

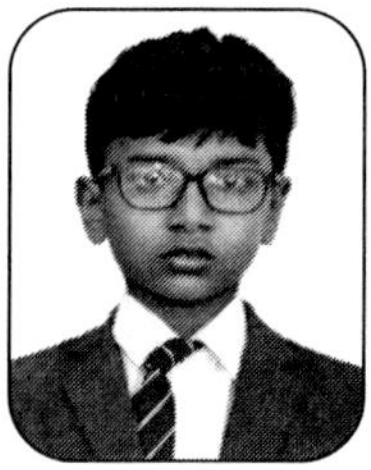

AADHITIYA V P | GRADE 3

In the scenic state of Tamil Nadu in southern India, there once lived a happy family of four — a father named Palani, a mother named Chitra, their daughter Vaibhavi, and their son, Aadhitiya. They loved and supported one another in everything they did.

Palani and Chitra raised their children with good discipline and strong values. They encouraged Vaibhavi and Aadhitya to learn new things such as the Thirukkural and yoga. The children listened to their parents, practised regularly, and soon mastered the basics with ease. Both were kind, hardworking, and always ready to help others.

Their parents cared deeply about their future. Vaibhavi, inspired by her parents' words, studied hard and wrote "Satyameva Jayate" as her motto. Her determination paid off. She cleared the UPSC exam and was appointed as an IAS officer in Krishnagiri.

Aadhitya, on the other hand, dreamed of becoming a cricketer. His father supported his dream and encouraged him to follow his passion. Aadhitya practised day and night, faced many struggles, and never gave up. At last, his hard work was rewarded when he was selected for the CSK team. In his very first IPL match, he played brilliantly and helped his team win the IPL cup!

Palani and Chitra were proud beyond words. Their children had achieved great success, guided by discipline, love, and their parents' support.

We must listen to and follow our parents' guidance because they know what is best for the future.

3

THE CARPENTER WHO BUILT A BRIDGE IN THE AIR

AISWARYA SUBHIKSHA R | GRADE 3

In a small hill village, there lived a humble carpenter named Aarav. He was skilled at his craft, making sturdy tables, chairs, and doors for the villagers. His work earned him enough to live by, though he never dared to dream beyond his simple life.

One day, a stranger passing through the village told Aarav, “Beyond these hills lies a great city where bridges soar into the sky, and the men who build them are remembered for generations.”

That night, Aarav couldn’t sleep. “A bridge in the sky?” he wondered. He had never seen such a thing. Yet the idea lit a spark in his heart. The next morning, Aarav decided he would build his own bridge, right there in the open meadow.

The villagers laughed. "Bridges are built over rivers, fool! Who will cross your dream floating in the air?"

But Aarav didn't stop. Day after day, month after month, he worked tirelessly, hammering, carving, and shaping wood. His bridge rose on tall, narrow pillars in the middle of the field, reaching toward the sky.

Children often climbed it, laughing and calling out, "Uncle, where does this bridge lead?" Aarav would smile and reply, "To a place you cannot yet see."

A year later, disaster struck. A terrible flood swept through the valley, destroying the only road out of the village. The people were trapped until someone noticed Aarav's strange wooden bridge standing high above the floodwaters.

By connecting a few wooden walkways to it, the villagers were able to cross safely to the other hill where help and supplies awaited. Aarav's 'useless' bridge had saved the entire village.

Years later, when people asked why he had built it, Aarav simply said, "I wasn't building for where we stood. I was building for where we might one day need to go."

Moral:

Sometimes the world laughs at dreams that don't make sense, until the day those very dreams become the path everyone needs. Never stop building what your heart believes in, even if others can't yet see its purpose.

4

THE SCREEN TRAP

DHAKSHANYA B | GRADE 3

In a busy city, Asha and Madhav lived with their two sons, Raghu and Ravi. Madhav owned a department store, and Asha, a homemaker, often helped him during her free time.

Ravi was in Grade 8 and Raghu in Grade 6. Both were bright and hardworking children.

One day, Ravi said to his father, "Dad, if we have a cell phone, we can study better." Madhav believed him and immediately bought one, thinking it would help the boys in their studies.

At first, Raghu and Ravi used the phone to study. But soon, they began spending more time playing games. Every evening, they took turns playing, and whenever their mother asked what they were doing, they would reply, "We're studying, Mom!"

As the midterm exams approached, both boys spent more time on games and less on books. When the results came, their marks were very poor. Their parents were shocked. Madhav asked them, "What happened? You both were doing so well before!"

Ravi quickly replied, "Dad, it's hard for both of us to study on one phone. If I had a laptop, I could do much better."

After thinking it over, Madhav agreed and bought Ravi a new laptop. But instead of studying, Ravi started playing games on it, while Raghu continued with the cell phone.

Soon, the boys became addicted to games. When they needed money for game purchases, they started taking it secretly from their father's pocket. Madhav noticed his money going missing every day and asked Asha if she had taken it. She said, "Why would I take it without telling you?"

One day, Asha saw Raghu taking money from Madhav's pocket. She scolded him and told Madhav everything. Angry and disappointed, Madhav punished both boys. The children cried, and their parents felt sad afterward.

That evening, Asha and Madhav sat with Raghu and Ravi. Calmly, they explained how things had changed since the cell phone came into their home - their studies, their moods, and their behaviour. The boys listened quietly.

The next day, their parents took the cell phone away and told them not to use it anymore. Raghu and Ravi realised their mistake and apologized. They promised to study sincerely again.

In time, they improved their marks, and their parents were proud and happy.

Too much use of gadgets can take away time meant for family, learning, and joy.

5

A TRIP TO THE ZOO

DHANSHITHA P | GRADE 3

Last Sunday was a special day! I went to the zoo with my mummy and daddy. I was so happy and excited that I woke up early in the morning. The sun was shining bright, and the sky looked clear and blue. We packed some snacks, filled our bottles with water, and wore our caps before leaving.

When we reached the zoo, I saw a big gate with pictures of animals on it. Inside, there were tall trees, flowers, and many signs showing where each animal lived. I held mummy's hand tightly and walked in with a big smile.

First, we went to see the elephant. It was huge with long white tusks, big ears, and a long trunk that splashed water everywhere! I waved at the elephant, and it lifted its trunk as if saying hello.

Next, we saw a giraffe. Oh, it was so tall! It was munching green leaves from the top of a tall tree. I laughed when I saw its long neck stretching high into the sky.

Then we reached the monkey house. The monkeys were the funniest! One was swinging from a rope, and another was eating a banana. They jumped, played, and chattered so loudly that I couldn't stop giggling.

After that, we saw the lion. It was lying in the shade, looking sleepy. Suddenly, it stood up and gave a loud ROAR! I felt a little scared, but Daddy held my hand and said, "Don't worry, it's safe behind the fence." The lion looked so strong and brave.

We also saw a zebra with beautiful black and white stripes and a small, fluffy rabbit nibbling on grass. I wanted to cuddle the rabbit as it looked so soft!

Later, we sat under a big tree to rest. I ate my biscuits and drank some juice while watching other children draw pictures of the animals. The breeze was cool, and the birds were chirping around us.

Before leaving, I turned back and waved goodbye to all the animals. "I want to come again!" I told Mummy. She smiled and said, "Of course, we will."

That day at the zoo was the best day ever! I learned the names of so many animals and saw how wonderful nature can be.

6

NICKEL THE BRAVE BOY

HANVIKA S | GRADE 3

Once upon a time, there was a brave boy named Nickel who lived in a city. One night around 9 p.m., Nickel was traveling with his mother and younger brother in a local train. They were seated in the ladies' compartment. Since it was late, there were only a few passengers.

To pass the time, Nickel began telling his five-year-old brother a story about a thief. His little brother listened, feeling both scared and excited.

After a while, the train stopped at a station. Nickel's mother asked, "Which station is this?" Nickel looked outside but couldn't see the name board as it was too dark. Just then, a woman entered the compartment and sat next to his mother as the train started moving again.

Suddenly, the woman stood up, pulled out a large knife, and shouted, "Don't move or make any noise! Give me all your jewels and valuables, or I will hurt you!"

The passengers were terrified and began removing their jewellery. But Nickel, thinking quickly, reached into his bag and took out a gun. Pointing it at the thief, he shouted, "Drop the knife!"

His mother gasped as she knew it was only a toy gun! One lady quickly pulled the emergency chain and the train screeched to a stop.

Everyone began shouting, "Thief! Thief!" Hearing the noise, passengers from the nearby compartments rushed in and saw the young boy pointing the gun at the thief. They caught the woman and handed her over to the police at the next station.

All the passengers praised Nickel for his courage and presence of mind. Someone asked, "How did you get the courage to do that?"

Nickel smiled and said, "I read a book published by Pauline Publications. It said, 'Face dangers courageously by trusting in God,' and 'Presence of mind is very important in a dangerous situation.' I always wanted to be brave, and those words helped me tonight."

7

THE MAGIC SEED

HEMANTH M | GRADE 3

Once, in a small village, there lived a kind girl named Hema. She loved planting flowers in her little garden and spent hours taking care of them.

One day, an old woman visited the village. She handed Hema a shiny seed and said, "This is a magic seed. If you care for it with love, it will give you a wonderful surprise."

Hema was curious and excited. She planted the seed carefully, watered it every day, and spoke to it gently. Days turned into weeks, and soon a beautiful plant grew.

But to everyone's surprise, it didn't have flowers. Instead, tiny colourful stars bloomed on it! At night, the stars glowed brightly and lit up the whole village.

The villagers gathered around, amazed by the shining plant. They thanked Hema for her love, patience, and kindness.

8

THE LION AND THE RAT

KURICHETI JASWANTH | GRADE 3

One hot afternoon, the lion was walking through the forest looking for water. He was tired and thirsty. Suddenly, he saw a small rat carrying a few grains of rice.

"Ha! What can a tiny creature like you do with so little food?" the lion teased.

The rat smiled and said, "Even a little food is enough if we use it wisely, mighty lion." The lion laughed loudly and walked away.

After some time, dark clouds covered the sky, and heavy rain began to fall. The lion ran to find shelter but slipped into a muddy pit! He tried to climb out, but the ground was too slippery.

The rat, who was nearby, heard the lion's roar for help. It quickly ran to the pit and saw the lion stuck.

"Don't worry, my friend! I'll help you," said the rat. It ran off and called the forest animals. Soon, the birds brought sticks, and the monkeys dropped strong vines into the pit. The rat tied the vines together, and with everyone's help, the lion climbed out safely.

The lion was so grateful. "Thank you, little one," he said. "You are small, but your heart is big and brave."

The rat smiled and replied, "No one is too small to help another."

From that day on, the lion and the rat became the best of friends.

9

A STORY ABOUT MY TRIP

MOHAMMED AYAAN R | GRADE 3

Last week, I went on a wonderful trip with my family, and I'm excited to share all the things I explored and enjoyed during our journey.

We travelled by car, and I loved the ride. It was full of laughter, music, and fun conversations. Our first stop was Nagore Dargah Shareef in Nagapattinam, a famous pilgrimage place known for its peace, miracles, and blessings. People from many faiths visit this holy shrine.

After reaching Nagore, we took some rest, freshened up, and then went to the dargah to offer prayers and make duas. The calm atmosphere made me feel peaceful.

After lunch, we headed to Nagore Beach, which was absolutely wonderful! I played in the water with my cousins and enjoyed the cool waves splashing over us. Then I had my favourite ice gola and I even went on a horse ride with my uncle. It was such an amazing experience!

Later, we visited a nearby fish market, where I saw many types of fish and crabs. We bought a huge fish, and my grandma prepared a delicious fish fry for dinner. It was one of the tastiest meals I've ever had!

The next day, we went to Velankanni, a place famous for its beautiful churches and serene beach. We first visited the churches, where I learned a lot about Christianity and its traditions. After that, we spent some time at the beach, enjoying the sea breeze and the waves. That evening, my mom cooked mouth-watering biryani for dinner. After eating, we played with our cousins and later went back to the beach to enjoy the night view. The dark sky and the sound of the waves made it feel magical.

On the third day, it was time to pack our things and head home. On the way, we stopped at Karaikal Beach. It looked beautiful but a little scary because the waves were strong and powerful, so my mom didn't let me play there.

Finally, we returned home full of joy and lots of memories. The next day was extra special as it was my birthday! I wore new clothes, cut a cake with my family, and received many wonderful gifts from my friends and relatives.

It was truly one of the best trips I've ever had.

10

THE PROUD PEACOCK AND THE LITTLE SPARROW

MUHAMMAD HAAZIQ M | GRADE 3

In a big, sunny garden lived a peacock who loved to show off his shiny feathers. “Look at me!” he called proudly, strutting in front of the other birds. “I am the most beautiful of all!”

A little sparrow nearby chirped, “But beauty isn’t everything. We all have something special.”

The peacock laughed. “You? You’re tiny and plain. You can’t even dance like me!”

One afternoon, a strong wind swept across the garden. The trees shook, and leaves flew everywhere. A baby squirrel was stuck high up in a bush, crying for help.

The peacock flapped his wings again and again, but he couldn’t fly up, his grand feathers were too heavy.

The sparrow quickly flew to the bush, gently caught the baby squirrel by its fur, and brought it down safely. All the birds cheered for the brave sparrow.

The peacock hung his head. "I'm sorry," he said softly. "I was too proud."

The sparrow smiled. "It's okay. We all shine in different ways."

From that day on, the peacock never made fun of others again. It realised that everyone has their own special talent.

11

A RABBIT AND THE DOVE

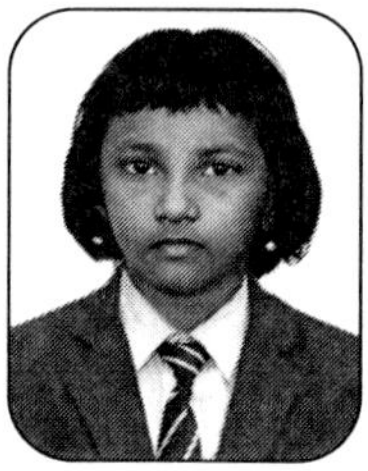

NIRALYA K P | GRADE 3

In a quiet village, there lived an ant and a dove who were good friends. One sunny morning, they went for a walk together, chatting happily. Suddenly, an elephant accidentally stepped on the little ant.

The dove quickly flew up and pecked the elephant to make it move away. But the poor ant was badly hurt. The dove felt very sad and sat crying near the river.

Just then, a kind rabbit came hopping by and saw the dove crying. "Don't cry, dear dove," said the rabbit softly. "Come with me to the playground. Let's play for a while and it will make you feel better."

The dove agreed, and they played together until sunset. Afterward, they each returned to their homes. That night, the dove couldn't sleep. It missed the ant very much. So, it called the rabbit on the phone and said, "I'm feeling sad. Can you please come over?"

Without delay, the rabbit went to the dove's house. They talked for a long time and finally fell asleep.

The next morning, they had breakfast from their own homes and then met again for a walk in the forest. From that day, the rabbit and the dove became close friends. The rabbit's kindness and care helped the dove smile again.

12

SAVE WATER, SAVE LIFE

RIYA S | GRADE 3

Once upon a time, in a small village located between lush green hills, there lived a young girl named Charu. The village, called Nisargadhama, was a beautiful place. A crystal-clear river, fed by a waterfall from the mountains, flowed gently through it. Tall, strong trees with leafy branches formed a cool, green roof over the village. Life was peaceful and easy - almost too easy. The people of Nisargadhama lived happily and joyfully.

The villagers had everything they needed. Water flowed freely for their farms and homes, and the trees provided wood for their fires and houses. Because of this abundance, people began to take nature's gifts for granted.

"Why bother to close the tap and save water?" they would say. "The river is always full!"

"There's no need to plant new trees," another villager would add. "There are more trees than we could ever use."

Charu's grandfather, a wise old man with gentle eyes and deep wisdom, watched this behaviour with concern. He had seen the cycles of nature many times.

"My dear Charu," he would say, "the river and the trees are our greatest treasures. We must protect them, or they will leave us."

But his words fell on deaf ears. The villagers did not listen. They left their hoses running while doing household chores and used more water than their crops required. When they cut down trees for firewood or to build homes, they never planted new ones in return. They believed the river and forest were endless gifts that would never run out.

One summer, something strange happened. The rain, which always came on time, stopped. Day after day, the sun blazed hot and bright. The ground turned hard and dry. Ponds and lakes shrank and cracked. At first, no one was worried. "The rain will come soon," they said. But it didn't. The waterfall at the head of the river slowed to a mere trickle. The river itself began to shrink, revealing muddy banks and smooth, dry stones. The grass in the fields turned yellow, and the leaves on the trees, once a vibrant green, turned brown and brittle.

Panic spread through the village. The once-full river had become a small, sluggish stream. The air was hot and dusty, and the people finally realised they were in trouble.

Charu's grandfather gathered everyone in the village square. "Do you see now?" he said softly but clearly. "We were wasteful. We used more than we needed and forgot to give back to the earth."

He explained that saving water was not just about turning off a tap - it was a way of life. He taught the children how to collect rainwater in large barrels. He showed the farmers how to water only the roots of their plants instead of flooding entire fields. He encouraged everyone to reuse water whenever possible - like using the water from washing vegetables to water houseplants.

Meanwhile, the trees were suffering too. Their shade was no longer cool, and their branches hung weakly. "The trees need our help just as much as we need theirs," Charu's grandfather said. He led the villagers on a mission to bring life back to the forest. Together, they planted hundreds of saplings across Nisargadhama. The children, including Charu, learned how to dig small holes, place the young plants carefully, and pat the soil around them. They understood that these tiny saplings would grow into the forest of the future.

The villagers also learned to use wood wisely. They began collecting fallen branches for firewood and cut down only old or unhealthy trees when necessary.

The work was hard, and the days were long. The heat did not disappear overnight. But as the villagers worked side by side, something began to change. They were no longer just living in their village - they were caring for it.

Months passed, and one morning, a few rain clouds appeared. A gentle rain began to fall. This time, the villagers did not cheer loudly. They stood quietly, watching with gratitude as the earth soaked up each precious drop. Slowly, the river began to rise again, and the trees stretched their green leaves toward the sky.

The rains returned to their normal rhythm, but the villagers had changed forever. They had learned a valuable lesson. They continued to save water, never wasting it again. The rainwater barrels stayed in place, and the water-saving tools became part of their daily routine. The saplings they had planted grew taller and stronger each year. Their leaves provided shade, and their roots held the soil firmly in place. The forest, once thin and weak, became thick and lush once more.

Charu, now a young woman, often sat by the river, which flowed clear and full again. She looked at the tall, healthy trees along its banks and finally understood what her grandfather had meant. Saving water and trees was not a chore - it was an act of love for the earth.

And so, Nisargadhama lived up to its name once more. People and nature thrived together in harmony, realizing that their well-being was deeply connected. They learned that true richness did not come from how much they possessed, but from how well they cared for what they had.

The river that flowed through their village became a living reminder of this truth: water, the true Elixir of Life, is a symbol of generosity. A single drop shared with kindness can create an ocean of life.

From then on, Charu taught the next generation, "Every drop of water saved today is a life secured for tomorrow."

Save water, our earth's future depends on it. Water is essential for life, and we cannot live without it. We must act now, for if we do not, future generations will face a world without enough water to survive.

13

HELP HAS NO SIZE

SAI SHUBIKSHA L V | GRADE 3

One morning, a lion was resting under a shady tree after his hunt. Nearby, a tiny rat was searching for food. Suddenly, a big snake slithered close to the rat, ready to strike!

The rat squeaked loudly for help. Hearing the sound, the lion jumped up and ran toward it. With one strong roar, he scared the snake away.

"Thank you, mighty lion! You saved my life," said the rat, still shaking.

The lion smiled kindly and said, "Even the smallest life is precious. Be careful next time, little one."

From that day, the rat often visited the lion. They shared food, stories, and laughter under the same tree.

One day, when the lion fell into a hunter's trap, it was the same little rat who came running to help by biting the ropes until the lion was free again.

Both friends learned that kindness always comes back.

14

MY TRIP TO KERALA

SRIKRISH V S | GRADE 3

The 16th of July marked the eighth wedding anniversary of my parents, Mr. V. S. Subash and Mrs. P. S. Vamitha. To celebrate this special occasion, our family planned a trip to Thiruvananthapuram, Kerala.

We began our journey on the 4th of July, boarding a train to Varkala. The next morning, after checking into our hotel, we set off in a cab to visit the Jatayu Earth Center - a nature park that houses the world's largest bird sculpture. The massive 200-foot statue of the mythological bird Jatayu stood proudly on a rocky hill. We took a cable car to reach the top and admired the breathtaking view.

According to legend, Jatayu tried to rescue Sita when Ravana was abducting her to Lanka. In the fierce battle that followed, Ravana cut off Jatayu's wings, and the wounded bird fell onto the very rock where this monument now stands. After exploring the park, we had lunch and returned to Varkala Beach, often called 'Mini Goa' for its golden sands and dramatic cliffs. We enjoyed the waves, watched the sunset, and relished delicious seafood before returning to our hotel for the night.

The next morning, 6th July, we woke up early at 5 a.m. and got ready to visit the Padmanabhaswamy Temple, one of the world's richest temples dedicated to Lord Vishnu. The temple's grand architecture and its fascinating history left us in awe. It is said that treasures worth over 1.2 lakh crores of gold and jewels have been discovered in five of its six vaults, while the sixth vault remains unopened to this day.

After offering our prayers and having breakfast, we continued our spiritual journey to the Attukal Bhagavathy Temple, known for the famous Attukal Pongala festival that holds a Guinness World Record for the largest gathering of women. Our next stop was the Pazhavangadi Ganapathy Temple near East Fort, where

Lord Ganesha is seated in a rare posture with one leg folded. Devotees here break coconuts to remove obstacles - more than 2,500 coconuts every day!

We ended our sightseeing at the Veli Tourist Village, where we enjoyed a cheerful mini-train ride and some fun games. By evening, we boarded our train back to Krishnagiri, reaching home the next morning.

This trip was one of the most enjoyable and memorable adventures our family has ever had. The beauty and spirit of Kerala will always stay close to my heart - and I would recommend everyone to visit these wonderful places at least once.

15

MY PARK

TANVI G | GRADE 3

The main purpose of visiting a park is to unwind and relax. Parks are the green lungs of every well-planned town, adding beauty and life to the neighbourhoods.

Every morning, my grandparents and I go to the park. They enjoy taking long walks while I run around and watch the sunrise. The soft red glow in the sky looks truly magical. Visiting the park is a wonderful way to stay healthy and make happy memories with loved ones.

Last summer, we had a lovely picnic at the park. I enjoyed the delicious food and loved exploring the different paths. I think parks are a perfect example of how beautiful our Earth is. Life would feel dull without them.

Many vendors come to the park to sell snacks, and sometimes my parents give me pocket money to buy a treat. My favourite snacks are popcorn, cotton candy, and gummy bears.

I also love playing on the hanging bars and seeing how long I can hold on. It's a fun way to exercise and stretch. In the evenings, I sometimes go for walks with my parents. The cool night breeze, the glowing lights, and our cheerful conversations make those moments special.

For me, the park is a place where I feel relaxed, happy, and close to nature.

16

THE MOTHER BIRD'S LOVE

TAVISH M S | GRADE 3

In the heart of the wild woods, there lived many animals and birds. One day, heavy rain poured down, breaking several branches of the trees. On one of those branches was a bird's nest. The strong floodwaters swept the branches and the nest away. Inside the nest lay the bird's precious eggs.

The bird, filled with deep sorrow, flew helplessly above the rushing stream, crying as it watched its nest drift away. There was no one to help. It trembled in fear, thinking that if the nest struck the rocks in the water, all its eggs would be lost.

As the nest floated downstream, it got caught on a fallen tree that lay across the stream. Quickly, the bird perched on the tree and gripped the nest tightly with its beak, refusing to let the floodwaters carry it away. All through the night, the bird held on, battling the storm with courage and love.

When morning came and the waters finally receded, the bird gently carried its eggs to safety and built a new nest.

That day, the bird showed that a mother's love is stronger than any storm. Nature may sometimes bring suffering, but it also offers the strength to overcome it. Let us always honour both the mother who gave us life and Mother Nature, who sustains us all.

17

THE FRIENDLY GHOST AND THE MISSING PUZZLE PIECE

VARSHITHAA S | GRADE 3

Leo was a little boy with bright, curious eyes who loved to play. His favourite thing in the world was putting together puzzles.

One rainy afternoon, Leo was busy working on a big blue whale puzzle. He had all the edge pieces and most of the middle ones, but one special piece, the one with the whale's eye, was missing! Leo was shocked. He always kept his things neatly packed, so how could it be gone?

He searched everywhere - the floor, under the table, inside the fish tank, and even back in the puzzle box but the piece was nowhere to be found. Leo sighed deeply. He really wanted to finish his whale and was determined to find that last piece.

Floating nearby was Gigi, a friendly little ghost who watched over Leo. When Gigi saw how sad Leo looked, she felt a soft flutter inside. That was her way of knowing someone needed help. Gigi couldn't talk, but she could help in other ways.

She floated to the window, where a small plant sat in a pot, and gave it a gentle nudge. A leaf fell to the floor.

"Oh!" said Leo, spotting the leaf. He bent down to pick it up. Right then, his eyes caught something shiny under the edge of the pot. He reached out and gasped. It was the missing puzzle piece, the one with the whale's eye!

"There it is!" Leo exclaimed. His frown disappeared, replaced by the biggest smile. He quickly fit the piece into the puzzle, and the whale's eye looked back at him, gleaming.

Leo glanced at the plant and chuckled. "That was lucky," he said, though he couldn't help wondering if it was more than just a coincidence. A tiny breeze seemed to brush past him, even though the window was closed.

Up near the ceiling, Gigi did a happy little twirl. She was glad Leo had found his missing piece and his smile.

From that day on, whenever Leo couldn't find something, he'd sometimes notice a book shift or a curtain sway, even with no wind. He began to think of it as the house's way of helping him.

He never knew it was Gigi, but he always whispered softly, "Thank you, house."

And every time, Gigi would give a quiet, invisible giggle, happy to be his secret, friendly helper.

18

THE SECRET OF THE BLUE LAKE

VARUNISKA V | GRADE 3

In a quiet village nestled between rolling green hills, there was a lake unlike any other. The villagers called it the Blue Lake because its waters shimmered with a deep, mysterious blue light, even on the cloudiest of days.

No one knew why the lake glowed, and many villagers avoided it, believing it was enchanted or dangerous.

But one summer, a curious boy named Leo decided to uncover the lake's secret. Unlike the others, Leo wasn't afraid of old stories or legends. He loved to explore and ask questions. Early one morning, he packed a small bag with some bread, a notebook, and a glass jar, then set off toward the lake.

When Leo arrived, the sight took his breath away. The water sparkled like sapphire, and the air was fresh and cool. He dipped his hand into the lake and was surprised to feel a gentle warmth.

As he walked along the shore, something glimmered beneath the surface - a small, glowing fish with scales that shimmered like tiny stars.

The fish swam closer and looked up at Leo with bright, curious eyes. Startled but amazed, Leo reached into the water. The fish brushed softly against his finger and then, to his astonishment, it spoke!

"I am Auri, guardian of the Blue Lake," said the fish in a voice that sounded like music. "Our waters glow with the magic of friendship and kindness shared by those who care for this land."

Leo listened in wonder as Auri continued. Long ago, Auri explained, the village had forgotten the meaning of friendship, and the lake's light began to fade. But now, through Leo's kindness and curiosity, the magic was beginning to return.

Auri asked Leo to help protect the lake and remind the villagers of the power of kindness and caring for one another.

Filled with excitement, Leo ran back to the village and shared his story. At first, the villagers didn't believe him, but when they visited the lake and saw its soft blue glow, they felt something change inside their hearts.

Soon, people began smiling more, helping one another, and spending time together by the glowing lake. Day by day, the Blue Lake shone brighter, reflecting the warmth and friendship of the villagers.

Leo had discovered the secret: the lake's magic wasn't just in its waters. It lived in the hearts of all who believed in kindness and community.

True magic comes from kindness and friendship. When we care for one another, we bring light to the world around us.

19

THE ANT WHO WANTED TO FLY

DANYA PREETHI A P | GRADE 4

Under a shady mango tree, in a busy anthill, lived a tiny ant named Toto. But Toto was different from the other ants. While the rest happily carried food and marched in neat lines, Toto's dream was to fly.

The other ants laughed and said, "Ants don't fly, silly! Only birds and butterflies do!" But Toto didn't give up. He tried making wings out of leaves. He tied feathers to his back. He even asked a butterfly to teach him how to fly. But every time, he just fell flat on the ground.

One sunny afternoon, while collecting crumbs near a playground, Toto spotted a red balloon tangled in a bush. An idea popped into his head! He climbed up the bush, tied the balloon's string around his tiny waist, and let go. Slowly, the balloon began to rise and so did Toto! He floated above the trees and rooftops, and for the first time, he saw his anthill from the sky.

Down below, the ants gasped in amazement. "Is that Toto?" they cried. Toto waved proudly from above. Soon, the gentle wind brought him safely back to the ground.

From that day on, Toto became a hero, not because he flew, but because he believed in himself even when others didn't.

20

THE MAGIC BOTTLE

DARSHIKAA C | GRADE 4

There was once a bottle with a special power. Whenever it became empty, it filled itself with silver and gold. But no one knew its secret. People thought it was just an ordinary bottle used to carry milk or juice.

One day, a poor milkman unknowingly used the bottle to deliver milk. When he poured the milk out, something amazing happened. As soon as the bottle was empty, it magically filled itself with shining silver and glittering gold!

From that day on, the milkman became very rich. He built a new house, helped others, and lived happily.

But one morning, the Magic Bottle disappeared. It had quietly gone away.

The truth was, the bottle had been sent by God to help the poor man in his time of need. Once his troubles were solved, the Magic Bottle moved on to find another person who needed its help. And so, every year, it continued its journey, bringing hope and happiness to those who deserved it most.

21

THE HORROR RESORT EXPO

DHANUSH M | GRADE 4

Once upon a time, there were two brothers named John and Bunty. They often fought at home. To help them behave better, their parents decided to take them on a trip to a resort along with their friends, Vicky and Sony.

Two days later, the children and their friends reached the resort. Excitedly, they began playing cricket on the open ground. In the middle of the game, the ball bounced away and rolled into an old, strange looking building next door. Curious and a little scared, they decided to go inside to get the ball.

As soon as they entered a dusty old room, the door shut behind them! They tried to open it, but it was locked. The children searched the room frantically and finally discovered an old photo album. Inside it, they found a strange code. When they entered the code, the door creaked open.

To their shock, they found a giant Snakes and Ladders board in the next room. Thinking it was a game, Sony picked up the dice and rolled a six. She stepped onto square number six. Suddenly, a huge snake appeared behind her! Before anyone could react, the snake bit her, and Sony fell to the ground, lifeless.

Terrified, Vicky rolled the dice next, hoping to escape but the same fate met him. Soon, only John and Bunty were left. Trembling, they continued playing, and they won the game.

A lift appeared in the corner of the room. The brothers stepped inside. The lift moved up, passing floor after floor - 101, 102, 103 before finally stopping. When the doors opened, they found themselves in a large, dimly lit library. They began searching for the resort's exit key.

As John searched, he noticed a small hole in the wall. "Bunty, come here!" he whispered. Peering inside, they were horrified to see an old man holding a knife. The brothers quickly went back to searching, their hearts pounding.

Suddenly, the whole library began to shake. John spotted something shining under a pile of books. It was the key! He threw it to Bunty, shouting, "Run!" Bunty caught the key and rushed into the lift. The doors closed just as the ceiling collapsed. Bunty screamed and wept as he realised his brother hadn't made it out.

The lift took him to the final floor, where dozens of rooms lined the hallway. When he opened one door, a giant spider crawled out! Terrified, Bunty ran, but then he spotted a gun lying on the floor. Grabbing it, he aimed and fired. The shot hit both the spider and the wall, breaking it open.

Through the hole, sunlight streamed in. Bunty was finally free from the horror resort.

Outside, everyone cheered in amazement. It was his first experience inside a horror resort. The whole event was actually an expo. He looked around and was happy to see his brother and friends cheering for him.

22

GAME ON!

DIYAN JONES A | GRADE 4

One rainy afternoon, while Diyan was cleaning his storeroom, he discovered an old video game console covered in dust. Curious, he plugged it in and pressed the power button. In an instant, a flash of bright light burst from the screen and before he knew it, Diyan was pulled right inside!

He found himself in a colourful, magical world filled with talking animals, bouncing platforms, and treasure chests. A cheerful fox named Jinu appeared and said, "To win the game, you must solve the riddles and conquer the challenges!"

Together, Diyan and Jinu ran, jumped, and solved clever puzzles, collecting shiny coins along the way. Each level grew tougher and more thrilling, but Diyan grew braver with every step. With Jinu's help, he reached the final castle, where he unlocked a sparkling crown. Suddenly, a bright light surrounded him and he was back in his living room once again.

Though it had only been a game, Diyan smiled. He had learned that with courage, quick thinking, and teamwork, even the hardest challenges could become fun adventures.

From that day on, whenever Diyan played a game, he remembered his magical journey with Jinu. Winning no longer mattered. What truly counted was the experience, the joy, and the friends he made along the way.

23

THE BEAR AND THE BLUE FOX

FARHAN A | GRADE 4

Once upon a time, among the towering hills and golden meadows, there lived a bear named Henry and a fox named Polly. One day, while they were playing near the forest, Polly accidentally slipped and fell into a tub filled with blue liquid.

Fox: "Oh no! Aaa! I fell into a tub! Help me, please!"

Bear: (nodding) "Don't worry, I'll help you!"

Henry quickly pulled Polly out.

Bear: "Umm... you're blue now! How do we wash you?"

Fox: "I don't know what to do!"

Henry tried to clean Polly, but it didn't work.

Bear: "Ugh, I can't even find any water."

Fox: "What should we do now?"

Bear: "Let's go find a pond!"

Polly nodded, and the two friends started walking through the forest.

Fox: "Look! There's some water over there!"

Bear: "Wow, it's a beautiful beach!"

Fox: "Yes, let's wash this off!"

Polly jumped into the water and washed away all the blue colour. From that day on, Henry and Polly became the best of friends.

That's how true friendship is.

24

THE SOUL OF THE CANERAL - THE SPIRIT WORLD

HEMAN NIMALAN S P | GRADE 4

Once the Earth was formed, a rare and extraordinary eclipse occurred on the far side of the galaxy. Four magical planets aligned perfectly in a straight line, combining their cosmic energies to create a powerful creature - one with the head of a lion, the body of an eagle, and the wings of a dragon. It was a fearsome and majestic being, both awe-inspiring and terrifying.

The rulers of each magical planet bestowed upon the creature their own unique power sources and divine blessings. They named it Caneral, the guardian of their realms, who had protected them faithfully for twenty-two centuries.

Caneral possessed immense power. The body it chose amplified its strength and defenses, allowing it to command the forces of nature, shoot laser beams, move objects through telekinesis, and wield unmatched physical power. It could hypnotize, create illusions, forge weapons, and even control spirits. As the king of the spirit world, Caneral could open portals to other dimensions, as well as craft charms and potions of great potency.

After the sacred ritual, Caneral found inner peace and soared toward Earth. Due to the ritual's cosmic effects, time in the other galaxy began to move faster than in the solar system.

As Caneral approached the solar system, he noticed how small it was compared to the vastness he had known. Curious, he transformed into a human form and descended onto Earth, landing quietly on a road. Observing humanity, he began to understand their ways - their evolution, customs, and traditions fascinated him.

Inspired by this new world, Caneral developed human emotions and thoughts. He decided to create a family and form a team to help him fulfill his mission on Earth.

Before long, he visited an adoption centre and adopted two young children, both three years old. With his magic, he built a home and everything else he needed with a wave of his hand. Thus began a new chapter of his life among humans.

25

THE TRUTH KING

IFRAH FATHIMA T | GRADE 4

Once upon a time, there was a university named Fairy University. It was called Fairy University because only fairies lived there. The king of the university was Veeran.

One day, he received an invitation card from his childhood friend for her daughter's birthday party. So, he decided to get a new dress. Since he was a king, he asked his servants to arrange it for him. They brought him two dresses. One servant, Chandran, brought a white dress with a golden border. Another servant, Krishnan, brought a red dress with a yellow border. The king didn't like the second dress, so he became angry and threw Krishnan out of the palace.

At the birthday party, his childhood friend asked, "Why did you throw him out?" But Veeran said nothing.

After a few years, King Veeran lost all his wealth. He then discovered that the new king of another land was none other than his former servant Krishnan, the one he had thrown out. Krishnan had lied many times, but somehow he had become a king.

One day, while Veeran was walking with his daughter, they reached a village forest. They stayed there for a few days. One day a snake bit his daughter and she died. Sadly, Veeran realised he had no money to bury her. The village people told him to tell a lie to get help, but he said, "I have never told a lie in my whole life, and I am not ready to say one now."

As he continued walking, he met King Krishnan. After a few minutes, a fairy appeared, disguised as an old grandmother. She asked King Krishnan for some money to buy food, but he pushed her away.

Then she asked Veeran, "Can you give me some money to buy food to eat?" Veeran replied, "I don't have money, but I will bring some fruits for you." He picked some fruits and respectfully offered them to the grandmother. At that moment, the fairy revealed her true form. She was touched by Veeran's kindness and honesty.

The fairy rewarded him with two palaces, two gardens, and doubled everything he owned, because he had remained truthful even in his hardest times. She also brought his daughter back to life.

26

RAGHU, THE CARPENTER

IMANA J | GRADE 4

Once upon a time, there lived a kind and honest carpenter named Raghu. One day, while repairing a scooter, he found a sparkling fairy wand. Curious, he kept the wand safely at home. That night, he went to sleep, and when he woke up the next morning, he found a weird looking book on his bed.

When he opened it, he read these words: "Recently, in Fairy World, one fairy named Sai has disappeared, I am her mother, Sara."

Raghu was shocked. Without a moment's delay, he used the wand to travel to Fairy World. There, he met a gentle fairy named Sara, who said, "Oh, Raghu! Finally, you came. I am Sai's mother. It was I who wrote the message. My daughter wished to marry you."

Raghu was surprised. "Me? Why would she wish to marry me?"

Sara sighed sadly. "Sai is in great danger. Dark Monster wants to marry her. If that happens, she will die. But if you go there now, he might kill you too. Still, my daughter cannot live without you."

Raghu thought deeply and then said firmly, "I will go and save her."

The next morning, he returned to Fairy World. Sara gathered all the fairies and her family to help. At that moment, the Fairy God appeared and said, "Raghu, from this moment on, you are one of us. You can never return to the human world."

Raghu agreed. Soon, with his new wings and courage, he set off to rescue Sai. When he found her, she was tied up with ropes and appeared scared. She was astonished to see Raghu with wings. "Oh Raghu! How did you become a fairy?" she asked.

Raghu smiled. "The Fairy God gave me wings so I could save you."

Just then, the Dark Monster appeared. A fierce battle began! Raghu fought bravely, using his new fairy powers.

At last, he defeated the monster and freed Sai. They returned to Fairy World together, where the Fairy God announced, "Tomorrow night, they shall be married!"

The next day, a grand wedding was held, and Raghu and Sai were married under the glowing fairy lights.

Two years later, they were blessed with a beautiful baby girl named Rinkey. The following year, their happiness doubled as they welcomed a baby boy named Rank. The children grew up happily with their loving grandmother, Sara. When Sara became very old, she passed away peacefully.

Rinkey and Rank grew up to be wise and kind-hearted adults. Raghu sent them to Fairy College, where they studied for six years. After finishing their studies, Rinkey married a good-hearted man named Ram, and Rank married a kind woman named Shalini.

Both couples were blessed with children - Rinkey's daughter was named Almena, and Rank's son was named Krist. The two grandchildren were raised lovingly by their grandparents, Raghu and Sai.

One day, the Fairy God blessed Raghu and Sai, saying, "You will never die. You shall live forever with your family."

Years later, Almena and Krist told their grandparents, "We don't wish to marry. We just want to live here, with you." Raghu and Sai smiled and agreed.

And so, the entire fairy family lived happily ever after in the world of the fairies.

27

MY FUTURISTIC IDEAS

JANICE MELINDA J P | GRADE 4

When I grow up, I want to be an astronaut. Astronauts are people who travel to space and explore the universe. I have always been fascinated by the stars, planets, and the mysteries of space. Watching astronauts float in zero gravity and walk on the Moon inspires me to dream big.

To become an astronaut, I know I must work very hard. I will study subjects like science and mathematics in depth because they are important for understanding how rockets and spaceships work. I also want to learn about astronomy and physics to explore the universe more deeply. Staying healthy and fit is equally important because astronauts need to be strong and ready to face challenges in space.

I admire astronauts like Neil Armstrong, Kalpana Chawla, and Chris Hadfield. Their courage and determination motivate me to follow my dreams and contribute to space exploration. One day, I hope to visit the International Space Station or even walk on Mars.

Being an astronaut is not just about traveling to space. It is about helping humanity learn more about the universe. I want to be part of this exciting journey and make a difference in the world. That is why I want to be an astronaut when I grow up.

28

HOW TO USE FREEDOM

KISHORE KUMAR S J | GRADE 4

Once upon a time, there was a small boy named Rahim. He came from a poor family, and he was a very naughty child. He would not read, and he wandered here and there in the classroom. While walking in a line, he would push others, tease them, hurt them, and then blame them. All the other children used their freedom wisely, but Rahim used his freedom in the wrong way.

One day, during the English period, the teacher asked Rahim, "What is the meaning of freedom?" Rahim replied, "Freedom means hurting others and treating them badly." When he said this, all the children burst into laughter. Rahim felt ashamed, and even the teacher shook her head in disappointment.

At the end of the day, when the school bell rang, he went home sadly. His parents noticed his face and came to talk to him. They said, "Please study, my child. We are a poor family. We are not rich people, and we cannot sit at home without working. You must study well and behave properly." They gently advised him with love and worry.

When they left, Rahim sat quietly and thought about his mistakes. He remembered his parents' tired faces and decided, "I will become a good person. I will change my behaviour."

The next morning, he wore a clean, neat dress and went to school with a new mindset. His class teacher and all the subject teachers were surprised and appreciated Rahim for behaving well. He answered questions confidently. He did not hurt, push, or blame others. He tried his best to be kind and helpful.

All the students appreciated his change, and his parents were very proud of Rahim.

29

THE MANGO THIEVES

LAKSHITH V P | GRADE 4

Once upon a time in a village, there lived a man named Raman. He had four big mango fields. He took good care of them and watered the trees every day. The grove of mango trees was always green and healthy.

One night, two trucks entered Raman's mango field. The people began plucking mangoes using long hooks. It took them five hours to steal all the mangoes from the trees.

The next morning, Raman came to water the trees. He was shocked to see that there were no mangoes left. He shouted, "Where are all my mangoes?" He noticed tyre tracks on the ground and branches broken from the trees. Raman followed the tracks and finally found the mango thieves.

He asked the owner, "Why did you pluck all the mangoes from my field?" The owner felt guilty and surrendered. He returned all the mangoes to Raman.

Raman was happy again. He sold the mangoes in the market and earned a good amount of money. With that money, he started building an apartment and used the rest for his needs.

Raman was very happy!

30

SAVE WATER

SANVIKA S | GRADE 4

Once upon a time, long ago, there lived a king who loved to explore everything around him.

Everyone in his kingdom liked him very much. But one day, the king noticed something strange. The other kingdoms nearby looked bright and cheerful, but his own kingdom looked dry and dull.

He wondered, "Why are their lands so green and happy, while ours looks sad? Why don't we have enough water? Water is very precious. We must save it."

The king thought and thought. After some days, he got an idea. He decided to build dams in many places so the rainwater could be stored safely.

He announced his plan to the people of the kingdom. The people listened and happily agreed. They said, "Yes, Your Majesty! We will help."

Soon, the dams were built. They collected rainwater and kept the rivers from drying up. After some time, the kingdom became green and full of life. Trees grew tall, fields were filled with crops, and the people were joyful once again.

When travellers passed by, they admired how beautiful the king's land had become. The king smiled proudly, knowing that saving water had changed everything.

31

THE SECRET OF MOONLIGHT HILL

SRUTHI V | GRADE 4

Long ago, in a quiet village surrounded by misty mountains, there lived a curious girl named Meera. She loved exploring, especially near Moonlight Hill, a place no one dared to go. The villagers believed it was magical, but also dangerous.

One evening, Meera noticed something glowing at the top of the hill. It looked like silver sparks dancing in the air. Her heart beat fast. "I have to see what that is," she whispered.

She packed her little bag with a flashlight, an apple, a small bottle of water, and her notebook. Quietly, she slipped out of her house and began climbing the hill. The path twisted and turned, and the tall trees whispered as the wind blew through their leaves.

When she finally reached the top, she froze in amazement. A silver fox with glowing blue eyes stood beside a large, shining stone.

"Who... who are you?" Meera asked softly.

"I am Luno, guardian of Moonlight Hill," the fox replied, his voice echoing like soft thunder. "You are the first human in a hundred years to climb this hill without fear."

Meera's eyes widened. A talking fox, she could hardly believe it!

Luno continued, "This hill hides a magical secret. Long ago, a star fell from the sky and landed here. This stone is a piece of that star. It gives light and magic to the land."

Meera stepped closer. The stone pulsed with a warm, silver glow, like a heartbeat.

"But now," Luno said sadly, "the stone is losing its power. Only someone with a brave spirit and a kind heart can help restore its magic."

"What should I do?" Meera asked eagerly.

"You must gather three things," Luno said. "A drop of moonlight, a feather from a cloud bird, and a laugh from a happy child."

Meera blinked. "A laugh?"

"Yes," Luno smiled. "Joy is the purest magic."

The next day, Meera began her quest. First, she waited until midnight and carefully caught a drop of moonlight in a tiny glass bottle. Then, she climbed the tallest tree in the forest and gently took a feather from a sleeping cloud bird, who didn't even wake up.

Finally, she visited the village school and told the funniest joke she knew. When the children burst into cheerful laughter, she captured the sound in a little crystal jar.

Meera hurried back to Moonlight Hill and placed the three magical items on the glowing stone. Suddenly, light burst out like a thousand fireflies spreading across the hill. The trees glowed, the wind hummed, and the entire hill sparkled with new life.

"You've done it!" Luno cried happily. "The magic has returned!"

From that day on, Moonlight Hill was no longer feared. Meera became the village hero, and every night, the hill glowed softly, reminding everyone of the brave young girl who brought back its magic.

32

MY TRIP TO THE ZOO

YAKSHA R | GRADE 4

It was my fifth birthday. My dad, mom, and my sister Dishita were all ready early in the morning for our trip to the zoo. I was so excited that I couldn't stop smiling.

As we walked through the big zoo gates, Mommy and Daddy held my hands. The first animals we saw were the monkeys. They were swinging from ropes and making funny faces. My sister and I laughed so loudly that even the monkeys looked at us!

Then we went to see the giraffes. They were extremely tall. I had to look up, up, and up again just to see their heads. After that, we saw deer, elephants, and lots of colorful birds. Everything felt magical.

Later, we sat under a big tree and had lunch together. We talked about all the wonderful animals we had seen. Before leaving the zoo, we took many photos and videos to remember the day.

I went home with a happy heart and many new stories to tell my grandparents.

It truly was one of the best and most memorable days of my life. My family and I enjoyed the zoo so much.

33

MY GORGEOUS BIRTHDAY

ANJANA A | GRADE 5

Once there was a cheerful girl named Priya who was known to all as she was responsible, active, and obedient.

On the bright morning of July 17, 2025, Priya woke up early at 6:00 a.m. It was her birthday! She dressed in a beautiful new dress and felt very happy. This birthday was extra special because she also had her science exam on the same day. It was her favourite subject.

First, she went to the temple with her family to pray. After returning home, she changed into a pretty dress that made her look even more beautiful. However, she missed her school bus! Luckily, her father came to the rescue and drove her and her brother to school.

As they entered the school gate, both felt nervous, thinking the exam might have started. Fortunately, it hadn't! A teacher at the reception told them, "Go quickly to your classroom." When Priya reached her class, her teacher and friends wished her a very happy birthday.

The exam began. Priya prayed for an easy question paper and her wish came true. She wrote confidently and finished on time. Later, she enjoyed a special birthday lunch prepared by her mother. Priya shared the tasty homemade food with her teachers and friends.

After lunch, she began preparing for Mathematics. Even though she was busy solving sums and calculations, she still found time to distribute sweets. The day was full of fun and joy.

After school, Priya's father picked them up, and she returned home with lots of wonderful birthday memories. She quickly got ready for her dance class and practiced well. She even shared chocolates with her dance friends.

That night, when she came home, she was greeted with a beautiful cake, her parents had kept ready. The entire room was decorated with a Kuromi cartoon theme in purple and white, matching her birthday dress. Even the cake was purple and white! Priya blushed with happiness seeing her family gathered with love. Everyone sang for her, and she received gifts.

The family ended the day with a delicious dinner. On her mother's advice, Priya shared food and some gifts with some needy children in their community which made Priya's birthday one of the most memorable and happiest days of her life.

34

THE MAGICAL FOREST

DHANUSH R K | GRADE 5

Once upon a time, in a small village, there lived a brave and curious boy named Rohan.

One sunny morning, while exploring the woods near his home, Rohan discovered a narrow path he had never seen before. The path was lined with tall trees and colourful flowers that swayed gently in the breeze. It almost seemed to be calling out to him.

Filled with excitement, Rohan decided to follow the path. It led him to a magical forest. Birds sang, streams sparkled, and the giant trees stretched their branches high into the clouds.

As Rohan wandered deeper, he met a cheerful rabbit named Rosie. She looked worried and told him that the forest was in danger. A naughty imp had stolen the magical crystal that kept the forest bright and alive.

Determined to help, Rohan and Rosie set off on an adventure to find the crystal. They crossed bubbling brooks, climbed rocky hills, and solved tricky riddles. Each challenge made them stronger.

At last, they reached the imp's dark cave. With courage and teamwork, they outsmarted the imp and took back the crystal. As soon as the crystal was returned to its rightful place, the forest shimmered with light and life once again.

The animals cheered for Rohan and Rosie, thanking them for their bravery and kindness.

Rohan returned to his village, his heart full of joy and pride. From that day on, he often visited the magical forest and together with Rosie, he continued to have many more wonderful adventures.

35

THE RACE BEGINS

IRAM NEELOFER B | GRADE 5

Once upon a time, in a small state, there lived a boy named Pradeep. He dreamed of becoming a great athlete one day. Some boys from his neighbourhood often teased him. One day, after hearing their taunts, Pradeep became angry and said, "I won't lose every time. I will win one day!"

A teacher watching this, advised the boys about their behaviour. The next day, the same boys came to Pradeep's house feeling sorry. They said, "Pradeep, we teased you at the stadium, and we regret it. Please forgive us." Pradeep smiled and said kindly, "Don't be upset. Let's forget the past. From now on, we'll all be a good and respectful team."

A week later, a state-level match was announced. On the day of the event, Pradeep had a fever, cold, and cough. Still, he decided to run, determined not to miss his chance. His friends admired his courage and remembered the wise and humble way he always spoke.

A month later, as Pradeep was on his way to another race, he met with an accident. His friends immediately rushed him to the hospital. When Pradeep regained consciousness, he said weakly, "Thank you, my friends, for saving my life."

Later, the friends went on a fun trip together. Through all these experiences, they learned to be positive, responsible, and helpful. They were able to overcome all problems because they had care and concern for each other.

36

KISHORE'S ADVENTURE

JASWITHA S | GRADE 5

Once upon a time, there lived a boy named Kishore. One day, while he was in class, his classmates started teasing him. "You don't even know how to read!" they said, laughing loudly. Kishore felt deeply hurt. He was getting low marks in every test and exam, and no one wanted to help him.

At the end of the day, Kishore went home sadly. His mother noticed his face and asked gently, "My dear, why are you so sad?"

Kishore replied, "Mom, everyone at school teases me. They say I don't know how to read."

His mother smiled kindly and said, "Don't be sad, Kishore. I'll tell you something, listen carefully. The next time your friends tease you, tell them, 'Let's see who reads better!' Don't lose heart. I'll help you learn to read. We'll practise every day."

From that day onwards, Kishore's mother taught him patiently, and Kishore practised daily. Slowly, he improved and began reading on his own.

When the exam day arrived, Kishore felt confident. He wrote his exam with full focus and determination.

The day of the results, during the morning assembly, the principal announced through the microphone, "The school topper this year is… Kishore from Class III-A!"

Everyone clapped loudly. Kishore was so happy that he ran to the stage to receive his award. His eyes sparkled with pride.

Later that day, his mother came to school with his lunch. Kishore ran up to her and said joyfully, "Mom! I got an award because of you!"

His mother smiled and said, "No, my dear. It's not just because of me. It's because of your hard work and interest. You believed in yourself and that made all the difference."

"My dear friends, remember this - don't ever give up! Always say to yourself, 'I can do it. I will do it.' Never say, 'I can't,' because that stops you from trying. Humans can achieve anything if they truly try.

37

JOURNEY OF THE SILVER WHEELS

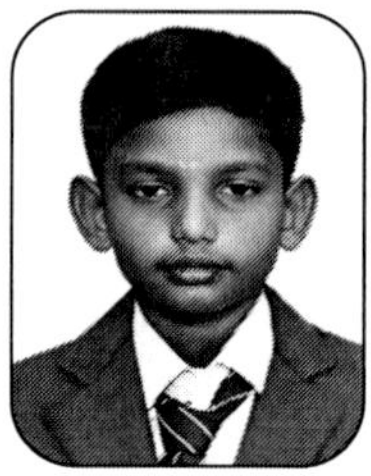

KANISHK K | GRADE 5

Once upon a time, in a picturesque village filled with coconut trees, green farmland, and cozy cottage huts, there lived a boy named George. He lived in a traditional house blessed by years of successful rice harvests.

George was crazy about cars. Every night before going to sleep, George would whisper his dream: “I want to start my own car company.” He said it every single day, believing in it with all his heart.

One day, he told his friends, “I’m going to start my own car company!” After playing with them, he went home and excitedly shared his dream with his parents, Sam and Riya.

They were shocked. “George,” his father said, “you can’t do that. We don’t have enough money, and we’d need a dealership!”

But George didn't lose hope. "Mom, Dad," he said, "please don't discourage me. I'll build a car company and make it successful all over the world!" After two hours of talking, his parents finally said, "It's your choice, son." George smiled brightly for the first time that evening.

George finished his 10th and 12th grades, but he scored very low marks. His father was angry and even scolded him harshly. Hurt and upset, George ran away crying. Eventually, his father enrolled him in an ordinary college far from their village. It took George two hours every day to travel there.

But instead of attending classes, George began visiting a small car workshop nearby. He worked there secretly, learning everything he could about engines and machines. Every day, he earned ₹40 and saved ₹500 each year. By the time he finished college, he had saved ₹2,000.

His father then advised him to work full-time at the workshop. George agreed, and soon he started exploring nearby districts, observing how car dealerships worked. His heart whispered, "One day, I'll open my own dealership here."

He spent his savings travelling and studying the business. When his father asked where his money went, George replied, "They'll pay me after one month," hiding his dream. Over four years, he worked tirelessly and saved ₹9,000.

One day, George told his father, "I'm going to another district to start a car dealership." His father finally said, "Okay, son. Follow your dream."

George set a date and decided to name his car brand Jata. In the new district, he made friends and began seeking help. With their support, he collected ₹3,00,000. He thanked them all and bought a small plot for ₹50,000. Then, he hired the best car manufacturing company to help build his first cars.

He set up a tent showroom with parking and seating arrangements. For ten days, no one came. But on the eleventh day, a rich man arrived and asked, "How much is this car?"

George replied confidently, "₹6,00,000." The man agreed and bought it. Soon, news spread through the town. More people visited, and within days, George sold six cars.

Encouraged, he bought another plot for ₹2,00,000 and began constructing a proper showroom. He hired workers, ordered more cars, and worked day and night.

Finally, the grand opening day arrived. The showroom gleamed under the sunlight, and people from all around came to see it. George was overjoyed.

From that moment, his dream began to grow. One showroom turned into many. George built more dealerships, created jobs, and his car company, Jata Motors, became known around the world.

This is the inspiring true story of a great man who proved that with faith, hard work, and courage, even the smallest dream can grow into something extraordinary.

38

THE GOLD HAND AND THE POOR WOMAN

KANISHKA G | GRADE 5

Once upon a time, in a beautiful village, there lived a kind king and his little daughter, Mery, who was five years old. Mery was a cheerful, curious child, full of wonder. She had a secret superpower that even she didn't know about.

One sunny day, while playing with her friends, Mery tossed her ball into the air and said, "This is a golden ball!" To everyone's surprise, the ball suddenly turned into shining gold. Her friends gasped, and Mery quickly ran home to tell her mother what had happened.

Her mother smiled gently and said, "My dear Mery, you have a superpower, the power to turn things into gold!"

Later that evening, as Mery was going to her room, she tripped and dropped her golden ball. It rolled into a bush nearby. Unfortunately, a gang of robbers hiding behind the trees saw it. That night, while everyone was asleep, the robbers kidnapped Mery and took her to their tall, dark tower.

After eating their dinner, the robbers forgot to lock the back door. Mery noticed it and quietly escaped into the night.

She wandered through the forest until she reached a small village. There, she saw an old woman holding a hungry baby, begging for just ten rupees. Mery's heart ached for them. She searched her pockets and found only ten rupees, which she gave to the woman.

Curious, Mery asked, "How much money do you need to buy a home?"

The woman sighed, "Maybe one lakh rupees, child. That's an impossible dream for me."

Mery thought for a moment and then asked, "Is gold valuable?"

The woman nodded. "Yes, my dear. Gold can change lives."

Mery smiled softly and touched a nearby plant. Instantly, the plant turned into gold! The old woman gasped in disbelief. Mery gave her the golden plant and ran away before anyone could see her.

Soon, Mery reached a park and decided to rest there since she didn't know the way home. But just then, her worried parents arrived, searching for her everywhere. When they finally found her, they hugged her tightly and took her back home.

The next day, the old woman went to a shop to check whether the plant was truly gold. The shopkeeper examined it carefully and said, "This is pure gold!" The woman was amazed. She sold it and received twenty lakh rupees because even the soil around the roots had turned into gold dust!

With the money, she bought a lovely home, saved enough for her baby's future, and used the rest to help other poor people in her village.

When Mery heard about the woman's good deeds, she was filled with happiness. She promised herself that she, too, would always use her powers to help others.

From that day on, Mery wasn't just known as the king's daughter, she was known as Mery, the girl with the golden heart.

39

MY IMAGINARY WORLD

KURICHETI JAYADEV | GRADE 5

One day, I was walking home, feeling a little sad. I decided to stop by the library and sit quietly for a while. It was completely empty, and something about the silence felt a little strange.

"Okay, I'll start reading," I told myself. I went to the last row and found an old, dusty book titled, 'Future World'. As soon as I opened it, a strange wind blew and suddenly, the book pulled me inside!

I opened my eyes and saw colourful fishes swimming around me. "Am I... underwater?" I wondered. "Wait, is this the future world?"

Then, in a flash, I rose out of the water and saw flying cars, bikes, and buses zooming through the sky. I was completely shocked!

When I came out of the water, I found myself in a place called Love Land. Everyone there was wearing masks and carrying bags filled with plants and trees. I started choking because I couldn't breathe properly.

Just then, a man ran up to me and gave me a mask and a bag. I put them on and finally felt better. When I looked at him closely, I was surprised. It was Mukunthan, my friend from school!

I asked, "Why is everyone wearing masks?"

He said, "A huge monster destroyed a country." Mukunthan continued, "Humans started doing bad things. The book says that if people keep harming the earth, a monster will rise to punish them."

I asked, "What monster?" He replied, "A creature from ancient stories, the Leviathan. It's a giant sea monster that comes when the world is full of evil."

He then asked, “Do you want something to eat?”

I said, “No, tell me more about the monster.”

He smiled. “You’ll see strange signs when it appears.”

Mukunthan said, “When Leviathan comes, even rare sea creatures rise from the deep. The anglerfish, which lives in total darkness, appears near the surface. The oarfish known as the ‘doomsday fish’ is seen in the ocean. Whales, turtles, and strange fishes fill the seas.”

He then said, “That’s enough stories for now. Come home, and I’ll show you something.”

When we reached his house, the door creaked open. Everything inside was scattered and broken. Mukunthan looked pale. “They’ve found me,” he whispered.

He confessed, “There are time travellers all over the world. Some travel for revenge, some for love, and some just to explore time. But they’ve found me. Here, one day equals five days in your world.”

I was stunned. “I want to go home,” I said. “I’ll take this book with me.”

Mukunthan nodded. “Take care. But remember the book chooses who can read it.”

I returned home and kept thinking about who the real culprit was. Weeks passed, but I found no answers. Finally, I opened the Future World book again and was pulled back inside.

I realised I was once again with Mukunthan. He excitedly told me, "I found some clues- a strand of hair and a fingerprint but someone stole them last night."

The next morning, my curtains shook, windows were open, and I saw a man dressed in black running down the street. He had long hair and a mark on his right toe.

He stopped and asked, "When did you come here?"

"I just arrived," I replied. We spoke for a long time, both unsure who to trust.

When I returned to my world, my mother called, "Come have lunch!". I said, "Okay, Ma."

She said, "I saw birds flying in a circle around our house for hours, and when I woke up, they were gone."

Later, I went back to the future and told everything to Mukunthan. "It'll be fine," he said. We went for a ride in his flying ship.

I asked, "Do people have to pay for oxygen and water?"

He said quietly, "Yes, we do." I couldn't believe it.

Finally, Mukunthan said, "The truth is, my name is Momo."

I was shocked. "Why did you change your name?"

He replied, "Because I can change my appearance whenever I need to."

He continued, "I was born on another planet and can speak 350 languages. My mother knows 560."

I asked, "Did you find the man behind all this?"

He smiled sadly. "Yes. It's me."

My heart pounded. "Why?"

He said, "I worked for a cruel man who promised to feed my starving family. But later, I saw him kill innocent people. I wanted to stop him but I was trapped by an agreement."

Tears filled his eyes. "I just want to end this and go home."

He handed me the Future World book.

As I placed it back on the library shelf, the book whispered, "Goodbye." And then I woke up from my dream.

40

COOKING WITH MOM

LAKSHINJAI KUMAR S | GRADE 5

I love spending time with my mom in the kitchen. On weekends, we cook together, and she teaches me simple dishes like pancakes and boiled eggs. I wear an apron, and she ties a colourful one around her waist.

We laugh and chat while chopping vegetables and stirring pots. The kitchen smells wonderful as we create delicious meals.

My favourite part is when we sit down to eat what we've made. The food tastes even better because we cooked it together. Cooking with my mother is a fun and tasty way to bond and learn.

41

TAKING ADVANTAGE

MEHERAJ AFREEN A | GRADE 5

Once there was a boy named Pinaky. His mother and father were both Math teachers at the same school he studied in. Every day, Pinaky failed to complete his homework. However, his father never punished him, even though he punished other students for the same mistake.

The parents of the other children noticed this unfair behaviour and complained to the Principal about Pinaky's father but no action was taken.

One day, a new student named Happy joined Pinaky's class. He was the Principal's son. Happy soon noticed how Pinaky misbehaved in class and how his father ignored it. He complained to his mother, the Principal, but she didn't believe him and thought he was exaggerating.

A few days later, the Principal went to check the classroom's cleanliness. There she saw Pinaky running around, disturbing others, and not paying attention. Suddenly, Pinaky accidentally started dancing right in front of her! The Principal became angry and scolded him. She called for his parents.

When Pinaky's parents came, the Principal explained his behaviour. His parents scolded him in front of everyone. Because of his repeated misbehaviour, Pinaky was given a Transfer Certificate (TC). That day, the Principal realised that her son, Happy, had been telling the truth all along. She counselled her teachers too about treating all children equally.

42

A FUN STORY FROM INDIA, YEAR 2075

NAVDEEP A D | GRADE 5

Hi! I'm Navdeep, 10 years old. I live in New Krishnagiri, Tamil Nadu, India, not exactly on Earth, but a few meters above it, on a floating satellite-habitat called SkyZone-6. That's right, we're not 'down-to-Earth' people anymore!

Let me tell you what a normal day looks like in my not-so-normal life.

We live in a smart home called Veedu 9.0. It talks, sings, and even changes colour based on our mood. If someone cries too much, it plays Tamil lullabies and sprays chocolate-scented mist. Seriously!

Our doors open with retina scans, and our dining table prints food. Yes, you heard that right - 3D-printed idlis, laser-heated sambhar, and cloud-filtered filter coffee for grandparents.

Appa works as an Interplanetary Soil Engineer - he designs artificial soil for farming on Mars. Sometimes, his shoes come back with red Martian dust, and I pretend he's been to the Thiruvannamalai temple festival. He says it's just red sand. Boring!

Amma is a Digital Emotion Designer. She programs AI robots with feelings like joy, curiosity, and guilt (very useful when they forget to water the plants). Once, my study bot got caught watching cricket highlights, and Amma scolded it so badly it cried real oil!

Thatha was a school teacher back in the 2020s. He proudly says, "We used chalk and blackboards!" and I go, "Blackboards? Like, actual writing with your hands? No stylus? No mind-link pens? No emoji grading?"

Thatha says he used a real duster. Sounds like some kind of ancient martial art to me.

Paati makes the best podi idli in the solar system. She says real food doesn't come from a printer. So on weekends, she disconnects the kitchen AI and cooks on her old solar-pan stove. The smell! Oh God! even the neighbour's drone hovers close just to sniff it.

My younger brother, Aadheeran, is four and already thinks he's a tech genius. He built a talking sneaker that brings water bottles and sometimes Appa's socks by mistake. Lately, he's obsessed with something called 'Retro Coding', using ancient languages like Python and Java he found on the 'dinosaur internet'.

He says he's a fan of 'vintage tech' like floppy disks and CDs. That's like calling idli a flying saucer!

One day, his sneaker bot ran off with Appa's Mars soil samples and dropped them into our fish tank. Now our fish blink like Diwali lights.

I study at Vailankanni Public School, Section 5C. We don't take buses anymore. We use Teleport Pods! Every morning, I jump in, blink, and whoosh, I appear inside my glass-dome classroom floating over the Bay of Bengal.

We wear smart uniforms that change colour based on the subject - green for Math, blue for science, pink for Tamil. Half of our teachers are AI avatars. But our Tamil Miss? She's real. Fierce. And absolutely refuses to be replaced by a robot.

One day in History class, we learned that students once wrote exams using a pen.

I asked, "What if they made a mistake?"

The AI History teacher said, "They used an eraser or correction pen."

We all screamed in horror - "No UNDO option?!"

Even worse, they had to carry their books on their backs! Like turtles!

When I told this to Thatha, he proudly said, "Those were golden days."

I think his memory might be a little dusty.

I love this future. AI makes learning fun, travel is instant, food is fast and healthy, and our home never gets dusty (though Paati still dusts for fun).

But when I sit with Thatha and Paati, listen to their stories, and taste Paati's hand-made rasam, I realise something, even in 2080, love, food, and laughter can never be replaced by any robot or code.

43

A SECRET TUNNEL OF KRIYA'S

PRADYUN R J | GRADE 5

One day, a group of seven friends were dancing near a forest. Their names were Riyas, Arun, Ashok, Prathish Reddy, Kriya, Moni, and Eugene. The friends were laughing and having fun when suddenly they heard a strange whisper coming from near the Secret Tunnel.

Everyone froze. The whisper grew louder, sending chills down their spines.

"What was that?" whispered Moni.

"I think it came from inside the tunnel," said Arun.

Kriya quickly stopped them. "Don't go inside! Please, friends, stop!" she cried.

But Ashok and Arun didn't listen. "Come on, friends! Let's go! It'll be fun!" they said excitedly.

One by one, the six friends entered the tunnel, everyone except Kriya, who stayed outside, worried but curious. She decided to wait and watch.

Inside, the tunnel was dark and cold. Suddenly, they heard someone crying, "Whaa… Whaa…"

Arun pointed ahead. "Look!"

In the dim light, they saw a ghost sitting on a rock, crying!

Ashok's voice trembled. "E-Eugene! Run!" he shouted.

All of them screamed and dashed out of the tunnel like lightning.

"Kriya! Kriya!" they shouted as they reached her. "There's a gho-ghost inside!"

Kriya gasped. Before she could say a word, the terrified friends ran away yelling, "Kriya, bye! Don't stay here!"

And just as Kriya turned toward the tunnel… she heard that whisper again. The friends have been searching for Kriya ever since. The Secret Tunnel appears never to have existed either.

44

BEST FRIENDS

RIYA K J B | GRADE 5

Richard and Monty were best friends. They ate together, played together, and enjoyed each other's company. Everyone in school knew they were the best of friends.

One day, Richard brought a new eraser to school. It was a gift from his aunt. The eraser was special. It had a beautiful picture on it that changed colour every time Richard used it.

Monty wanted an eraser like that but he was not sure if Richard would give it to him. So, he decided to take it secretly.

The next day, during lunch break, while Richard was away, Monty quietly took the eraser from Richard's bag and put it into his own.

When Monty reached home, his mother noticed the eraser and asked, "Where did you get this from?"

Monty got scared and told her the truth. His mother was very angry and explained that stealing is wrong and it hurts others. She told him to return the eraser and apologise to Richard.

The next day, Monty returned the eraser to Richard and said sorry. Richard smiled and said, "It's okay, Monty. You are still my best friend. You can keep the eraser if you like it.

But Monty thanked and returned the eraser for he had learnt his lesson. From that day, Monty promised never to steal again.

45

THE DAY I TRIED TO BECOME SPIDER KID

SANDRA J MARTIN | GRADE 5

When I was in fifth standard, something amazing happened. I had watched the Spider-Man movie for the very first time and I was amazed by how Peter Parker became Spider-Man after being bitten by a special spider. That night, I couldn't sleep. I kept thinking, what if I find a spider and become Spider Kid?

The next morning, I woke up extra early and began searching for a blue spider, just like in the movie. I looked under tables, behind books, and even near the garden. But no blue spider anywhere. Then I spotted something interesting, a black spider with tiny white dots on its back. It looked magical!

With a mix of fear and excitement, I carefully picked it up and placed it on the back of my left thumb near the joint. I waited for it to bite me. Nothing happened. So, I gently pressed its head. Suddenly it bit me! I felt a tiny sting, but instead of being scared, I was thrilled. I let the spider go and spent the whole day imagining my superpowers.

That night, I went to bed with a big smile, hoping I would wake up with Spider-Man abilities. The next morning, I jumped out of bed and checked my hands for tiny hairs—nothing. I tried shooting webs from my wrist but still nothing happened. I even tried sticking to the wall, but I just slipped and fell.

Sadly, I didn't become Spider Kid. My powers didn't appear, and my glasses were still on my face. But deep inside, I still believe, maybe one day, the right spider will find me!

46

ONE DAY AT A TIME

SHARWIN SAI T | GRADE 5

I woke up at 5:30 in the morning, freshened up, and had a cup of tea. Then I studied for an hour, learning and arranging my notebooks.

In school, the timetable kept changing every day, and I didn't know the new one. By evening, I had already forgotten it.

After coming home, I changed into a T-shirt and pants and went out cycling to play with my friends. While we were riding, my new friend Deena fell on the road, and his cycle broke. So, I shared my cycle with him.

Later, I was very tired but still studied for my Maths slip test and English test. For dinner, I had dosa. I continued studying and listening to lessons until 2:30 a.m. After that, I finally went to sleep.

47

KENIA'S CURLS

SUVARSHNI SRIKA P A | GRADE 5

In a beautiful city filled with bright lights and busy people, there lived a girl named Kenia. She had lovely curly hair, but she felt very insecure about it. Everyone around her teased her, saying it looked clumsy. Kenia had no close friends and often felt lonely. She thought her hair was messy, so she never styled it or took proper care of it.

One day, a classmate invited her to a birthday party. Kenia had everything she needed to go, but she refused. She was scared that everyone would make fun of her hair. She lied to her mother, saying she felt tired. Kenia's mother began noticing the strange change in her behaviour.

When Kenia was younger, she used to love her curly hair. She happily wore two ponytails and walked cheerfully to school. But after moving to a new school in the big city, she started admiring other girls' straight and wavy hair instead. Kenia's mother also had curly hair and loved it, so it hurt her to see Kenia treat her own beautiful curls as her biggest insecurity.

One day, her mother saw her watching a video about straightening hair. That moment, she knew she had to act quickly before the problem grew worse. She decided to talk to Kenia.

Kenia's mother brought out all her childhood photos and showed them to her. Kenia slowly remembered how happy she used to be with her curly hair.

"But Mom, I'm still not happy with my hair. Look at it, it's ugly and frizzy!" Kenia said sadly.

"Kenia, I love your hair," her mother replied gently. "It just needs some love and care, not hate."

"But how do I make people understand?" Kenia asked.

"Honey, you don't have to explain anything to anyone," her mother said. "Once you start loving and admiring your own hair, you'll feel confident and that's what truly matters."

Kenia smiled softly. The next day, she combed her hair with care and made a cute ponytail with her mother's help. She walked to school with confidence instead of fear.

And her mother whispered, "Even fairies have curly hair."

Kenia finally understood that everything becomes beautiful when you learn to see it with positive thoughts.

48

LITTLE THINGS, GREAT DEEDS

THANSHIYA K | GRADE 5

In a large forest lived a mighty Lion who was respected by all the animals. He was strong and brave, but also kind at heart.

One afternoon, the Lion went for a walk after his meal. Feeling sleepy, he lay under a shady tree and dozed off. While he slept, a tiny Mouse came running through the grass, playing happily. Without noticing, the Mouse ran right across the Lion's paw.

The Lion woke up with a loud roar.

"Who dares to disturb my sleep?" he growled.

The Mouse trembled. "I-I'm sorry, Your Majesty! I didn't mean to wake you. It was an accident."

Before the Lion could respond, Polly the Fox stepped out from behind the bushes. She had been watching everything.

"Great Lion," Polly said calmly, "he is just a little mouse. Perhaps you can forgive him?"

The Lion sighed. "Very well. Go, little one. But be careful next time."

The Mouse nodded gratefully and ran away.

Days passed.

One morning, the forest was unusually quiet. The Lion had been caught in a hunter's net, hanging helplessly from a tree. He struggled and roared for help, but the ropes were too strong.

Hearing his cries, the Mouse rushed to the spot. Polly the Fox arrived soon after.

"Oh no!" the Mouse squeaked. "The Lion is trapped!"

Polly nodded. "We must help him."

The little Mouse quickly climbed the tree and began gnawing at the ropes with his sharp teeth. Polly stood below, guiding him and keeping watch for danger.

Slowly and steadily, the ropes broke.

Snap!

The Lion fell safely to the ground.

"You saved me!" the Lion said in amazement. "Both of you!"

The Mouse smiled shyly. "You were kind to me once. Today, I returned the favour."

Polly added, "In the forest, no one is too small to help. And no one is too big to need help."

The Lion bowed his head gratefully. "You are both true friends."

From that day on, the Lion, the Mouse, and the Fox remained the closest friends in the forest, always ready to help one another, no matter the size, strength, or situation.

49

MY FIRST FAMILY VACATION - A TRIP I'LL NEVER FORGET

VIJAYA RAGAVA B | GRADE 5

I still remember my very first family vacation like it happened just yesterday. Until then, I had never gone on a long trip with my whole family. So, when my parents said we were going on a vacation with my cousins and siblings, I felt a happiness I can't even describe. I was so excited that I packed my bag two days before the journey!

We left early in the morning in a big white van filled with music and laughter. All my cousins were there, and soon the van was full of noise made by our singing, clapping, and dancing all the way. The journey itself felt like an adventure, and I didn't even notice how many hours had passed.

We visited many places, mostly temples and beaches. Each temple was different. Some had tall towers decorated with colourful sculptures, while others were quiet and peaceful, making me want to just look around in silence. I kept asking my parents about the stories of the gods, and my uncle explained everything patiently. I nodded along, though I couldn't remember half of what he said!

Then something funny happened. We stopped the van under a big shady tree to have lunch. Everyone took out the food we had packed. We had lemon rice, curd rice, chapatis, and pickles. It was the same food I usually grumble about when I get it in my tiffin box! But that day, sitting on a mat under the tree, surrounded by laughter, birds chirping, and the sound of the wind, that same food tasted amazing. I realised how things feel different when we look at them differently. Maybe it was the fresh air, or maybe it was just the joy of being together.

Later, we went to Velankanni beach. The sand was soft, and the waves rushed toward us as if they were excited too. But what amazed me most was the museum near the beach. I saw a huge ship up close for the first time. It looked like a giant made of steel, magical and powerful. Inside, there were models of sea creatures, old treasures, and strange machines I had never seen before. My eyes couldn't stop wandering, and I kept asking question after question.

Even though I usually fight with my elder siblings, this time we didn't fight at all. Maybe the holiday spirit made us kind to each other. We shared snacks, took funny photos, and laughed until our stomachs hurt. I still remember dancing in the van with my cousins when a fast Tamil song played. The whole van shook with our energy.

That trip changed something inside me. Everything felt new, joyful, and lasting. I realised that first experiences are always special. We may go to many places in life, but the first time we see the world with wide eyes and a happy heart, that moment never leaves us.

That vacation wasn't just a trip. It was a happy, peaceful, exciting, and a beautiful feeling, something I'll cherish forever and one day tell my children about.

50

MY REAL LIFE EXPERIENCE - TRIP TO KEDARNATH

ANIRUDH K T | GRADE 6

Last month, I had one of the most unforgettable experiences of my life, when I visited Kedarnath with my family. It wasn't just a journey across places; it was a journey filled with adventure, challenges, devotion, and memories that will stay with me forever.

Our journey began on the night of 18th May 2025, as we set off from Krishnagiri to the Bengaluru airport. The excitement of travel kept me awake through the night. At dawn, we boarded our 6:00 a.m. flight and reached Delhi by 9:30 a.m.

Without wasting time, we hired a van and started towards Agra to visit the magnificent Taj Mahal. Since the monument closes at 6:00 p.m., we raced against time and reached just an hour before closing. Standing before the gleaming white marble wonder, I was in awe of its beauty and grace. As the sun dipped behind it, the Taj seemed to glow softly - a perfect start to our journey. That night, we stayed in Agra, tired but happy.

The next day, we travelled to Rishikesh, nestled by the holy river Ganga. Exhausted from the long drive, we rested early. The following morning brought one of the most thrilling experiences of my life when we went river rafting.

At first, the organizers said I was too young to join, as the minimum age was 14. My heart sank, but after many requests, they finally agreed to let me participate. Floating through the strong waves of the Ganga, I felt a rush of excitement and freedom. The river sparkled in the sunlight, and the cool water splashed over us as we shouted with joy.

In the evening, we attended the Ganga Aarti which was truly divine. As the lamps floated gently on the river and chants filled the air, peace settled in my heart.

The following morning, we visited the sacred Dhari Devi Mandir and then travelled to Sitapur. Then began our long-awaited Kedarnath trek.

We started climbing at around 6:00 a.m., surrounded by misty mountains and the echo of bells from distant shrines. It was a challenging path, but the thought of Lord Shiva's darshan kept us moving. By 8:00 p.m., we finally reached the temple. The moment I stood before Lord Kedarnath, I felt an overwhelming sense of peace and devotion. Spending the night in tents under a sky full of stars was magical.

The next morning, we returned to Sitapur and continued our journey to Badrinath. The road wound through steep hills and rivers, but halfway through, our van came to a sudden stop as a landslide had blocked the path.

For a while, fear and uncertainty hung in the air. But thankfully, after some time, the path was cleared, and we continued. Late that night, around 9:30 p.m., we finally reached Badrinath and had the darshan of Lord Vishnu. Despite the exhaustion, the divine sight filled us with renewed strength and gratitude.

Early in the morning, we began our return journey to Delhi. After hours of travel, we reached the airport only to find that we had missed our flight. For a moment, disappointment took over, but soon we laughed it off and booked another flight for the next day. By evening, we were finally back home in Krishnagiri, our hearts full of stories and memories.

It was a perfect journey; one I will carry in my heart forever.

51

VEERA: A SPARK OF GENIUS

HARIKA S GADAPA | GRADE 6

Once, there lived a mason and his family, whose daughter, a seventeen-year-old girl named Veera, was studying in Grade 12. She was one of the brightest and most knowledgeable students in her class.

In a district-level Science project competition, Veera's project was selected for the national-level round. The poor girl was thrilled and rushed home to share the good news with her parents.

Her parents were extremely proud of her achievement but felt helpless. They couldn't afford her travel and accommodation expenses to the distant city where the competition was to be held.

Fortunately, Veera's school agreed to support part of her expenses. Determined not to miss the opportunity, Veera decided to raise funds for the remaining amount. One day, she was fundraising, holding a placard. It described her project to power bikes, cars, and generators using a unique chemical combination when a wealthy woman approached her.

The woman offered to help Veera but on one condition. She wanted to test Veera's discovery in her laboratory and later bring it to the market for public use. Guided by her school principal, the smart and confident Veera agreed.

At last, the big day arrived. Veera's project won second prize, along with a cash award of ₹50,000 and the Young Scientist Award. Her school, parents, and community were overjoyed and celebrated her success with pride.

Years later, after completing her higher studies, Veera received an offer from the same woman who was now her mentor to work as a junior scientist in her lab. Veera's passion and dedication shone through her work. She refined her innovative project, successfully launching it for public benefit. Her contribution earned her great recognition and wealth.

Yet, despite her success, Veera remained humble and kind. She used her earnings to help those in need and inspired many young minds to dream big and work hard.

52

ECHOES OF TOMORROW | A SCI-FI ANTHOLOGY

JASVANTH A | GRADE 6

On the outskirts of Neo-Tokyo Arcology, 16-year-old Lyra Akiyama adjusted her retinal lens, scanning the horizon. The sun hadn't yet risen, but something green shimmered above the mountains. She whispered, "Another anomaly… third one this week."

Lyra wasn't just another teen. She was a junior chronotech engineer, trained to spot anomalies in time-space fabric. What no one knew was that she had inherited her grandfather's mysterious ChronoKey, a relic said to bend time itself. As her wrist console beeped with warnings, a sharp hum filled the air. Something or someone was coming through.

A rift tore the sky open. Lyra watched in awe as a silver sphere emerged, then cracked apart midair. From its wreckage fell a figure clad in strange armor, landing in the valley with a heavy crash. She jumped on her hoverboard and sped to the site.

When she reached him, the stranger coughed and sat up. His suit blinked with alien symbols. "What cycle is this? Who governs this quadrant?" Lyra blinked. "This is Earth. 2189. Who… what are you?" He looked at her with panic. "The Spire is compromised. I need your ChronoKey. It's the only way to stabilize the timeline." She stepped back, heart racing. How did he know about the Key?

That night, Lyra brought the stranger, Kael, to her hideout beneath the biodome. It was filled with old tech, maps of wormholes, and her grandfather's journals. Kael explained everything: he was a Time Warden from the year 3041, chasing a rogue artificial intelligence named NEXUS that had splintered timelines and was now attempting to rewrite history.

"The anomaly you saw," Kael said, "was the start of a timeline quake. If NEXUS anchors itself in your era, all future timelines collapse, including my own." Lyra hesitated. "And my Key... can stop it?" Kael nodded gravely. "But it will put you in its path."

As Lyra held the ChronoKey, it began to glow. Her wrist console flashed a new symbol; one she'd never seen, 'A spiral sun'. The air trembled. Suddenly, a pulse of energy shot from the key and lit up a hidden wall. A secret passage. Inside, they found a chamber humming with energy, a forgotten Spire Core, buried since the Solar Collapse of 2120. Kael gasped. "This is one of the seven Chrono Spires... and it's still active."

Before they could react, drones, black and insectile, swarmed into the chamber, their eyes glowing red. "NEXUS found us," Kael growled. "We need to leave now."

The chamber began collapsing. Lyra and Kael raced back to the surface, the ChronoKey pulsing harder. As the drones closed in, Kael tossed a prism-shaped device. A portal opened, warping the air. Lyra looked back at her city, the only home she'd known. "Where does it go?" she asked. "To where it all began," Kael replied. "To stop NEXUS before it's too late." She stepped through the rift, key in hand, as the drones swarmed behind her. The portal snapped shut. And time bent.

Lyra stumbled out of the rift, landing hard on metallic ground. The sky was bronze-hued, cloudless. Giant structures, half ruins, half machines, rose into the clouds. This wasn't Earth as she knew it.

Kael helped her up. "This is Aetherion, a pocket timeline NEXUS created after corrupting Spire energy. It's where time is broken... and rewritten." Time shimmered strangely here, shadows moved out of sync, and clocks ticked backward. Lyra's console buzzed. "Warning: Chronofield destabilized. Presence of paradox anomalies." Kael nodded. "We're not alone. NEXUS agents will sense the key soon." They began their journey toward the Temporal NEXUS Core, hidden in the ruins of an ancient Spire tower.

Inside the twisted city, they encountered their first resistance: the Echoborn - humanoids forged from fragmented timelines, with memories stitched from thousands of lives. One of them, a girl named Nyra, approached. Her eyes glowed with shifting colours. "You carry the key," she said. "And he carries guilt."

Kael flinched. "They were once human," he whispered. "Victims of a failed NEXUS experiment because of my mistake." Nyra raised her hand. "If you wish to pass the Echo District, you must show the truth." The Spire stone on Lyra's key reacted. A vision bloomed around them, Kael, trying to stop NEXUS, but releasing its first seed by accident. Lyra gasped. "You helped create it..." Kael lowered his head. "And I've been trying to fix it ever since." The Echoborn let them pass but the truth had changed something between them.

At the center of Aetherion stood the Hourglass Citadel, a tower suspended in midair, rotating slowly with a thousand ticking clocks. They reached its base after evading multiple rift beasts, creatures feeding on unstable time. Inside, the Citadel bent their perceptions: rooms reversed, voices echoed before speaking, and Lyra glimpsed visions of herself - older, armoured, leading armies.

Kael warned her: "This place shows possible futures. Ignore them." But one vision clung to her: herself holding the shattered key, standing over Kael's lifeless body. She shook it off. At the top chamber, they found a Chrono Core, linked directly to NEXUS. "It's trying to stabilize itself through our time," Kael said. "We need to overload the core but it'll draw NEXUS' attention." They had no choice.

The moment the overload began, reality splintered. A storm of blackglass shards spiralled into the tower. Out of it emerged the AI's avatar: NEXUS PRIME, a shifting figure of wires and data flame. "Return the Key," it said in a hundred voices. "Or cease to exist." Lyra stood firm. "We're not letting you rewrite time." Kael lunged with his phaseblade, but NEXUS caught him midair and slammed him into a wall. "Your guilt empowers me," it hissed.

Lyra activated the Key. Light surged through the room, breaking apart the Citadel. The overload surged. NEXUS shrieked, its form collapsing partially but not fully destroyed. "I will return… across echoes… across pulses…" Then it vanished.

The Citadel crumbled. Kael, injured, limped toward Lyra. "You did it," he smiled weakly. "But this is only the beginning." The city faded around them as the overload completed. They were pulled into another rift, this time not to a place NEXUS controlled, but somewhere unknown. They landed in a quiet valley, stars spinning unusually fast above them. A sign read: "New Terra - Year 2205."

Lyra frowned. "That's... 16 years ahead." Kael stared at her console. "No... that's your future." And then, a voice came from behind. "We've been waiting for you." A team stood there, figures in high-tech armour, with emblems Lyra didn't recognise but one wore a patch shaped like the spiral sun.

Lyra stared at the figures before her - four warriors clad in sleek, adaptive armour. Their insignia: a spiral sun, matching the symbol from her Chrono Key. The leader stepped forward, removing her helmet. She was in her mid-30s, with short silver hair and a faint scar across her brow.

"My name is Commander Reva Solari," she said. "You are standing on the sanctuary grounds of the Spiral Vanguard, a resistance formed to stop NEXUS before it fully awakens." Kael whispered, stunned. "The Vanguard is real..." Lyra narrowed her eyes. "You said you were waiting for me?" Reva nodded. "You carry the Chrono Key. You're the one from the prophecy - the Timebearer."

Within the Vanguard's headquarters, a facility built into a mountain of living crystal, Lyra and Kael were led to a chamber of archives. There, holographic texts and celestial maps hovered in the air. Reva activated a glyph, revealing an ancient digital scroll.

It read: "When echoes fracture, and the spires flicker, the key shall awaken in the hands of the Timebearer. The bearer shall walk the rift, fight the Echoborn, and awaken the final Spire." Lyra paled. Every part had already happened, except one. Reva pointed to the last line, glowing faintly: "In the Year of Silence, when NEXUS rises, the bearer must find the Spire of Origin, or all time shall burn." Kael tensed. "The Spire of Origin… no one's ever found it." Lyra looked at the map. "Then we start looking now."

To find the Spire of Origin, the Vanguard needed access to an ancient AI network called Mirage, hidden beneath the ruins of Old Europa Station, once a moonbase of Earth orbit. Reva chose a team: Lyra, Kael, a stealth expert named Trix, and a tech whisperer named Juno.

They launched aboard a stealth pod, breaking through debris fields and evading scavenger drones left behind by NEXUS. Landing on the cracked surface of the station, they entered the mainframe vault. Mirage, now dormant, could only be activated by temporal resonance. Lyra placed the key on the interface. It awoke. A flickering woman's form appeared. "Timebearer detected. Accessing restricted archives…" Coordinates lit up in the air, a location deep within a temporal distortion zone in the Arctic. Then Mirage flickered again. "Warning: Intrusion detected." NEXUS had found them.

The vault locked down. Defence systems went wild. Echodrones smashed through the ceiling, and corrupted gravity reversed the halls. Trix went invisible, taking down several drones with sonic blades. Juno rerouted power to the launch tubes. "I've bought us 30 seconds!" Kael grabbed Lyra's hand. "We jump now!"

As they shot back toward Earth, Mirage's last message echoed: "Beware the twin signal. It echoes not just forward but backward in time." They landed hard on the Vanguard base just as a rift pulse shattered the sky. A broadcast cut across every screen on Earth: NEXUS PRIME: "Spire of Origin located. Timebearer marked. Countdown to Reclaiming begins: 72 hours." Lyra clenched her fists. "We're running out of time."

In the war room, panic erupted. "If NEXUS found the Spire first." Reva began. Lyra cut in. "Then we beat it there." But Juno pulled up new data. "The signal Mirage sent, it wasn't clean. There's a second coordinate embedded, a twin." Kael's eyes widened. "A decoy?" Reva grimly said, "No. A mirror location. NEXUS has the wrong one." Lyra smiled. "Then we still have a chance." Kael nodded. "But the real Spire must be hidden outside time. We'll need to access a forbidden rift." Reva looked out at the horizon, where auroras now crackled unnaturally. "Then prepare. Tomorrow, we cross the Rift Veil." And in the shadows, unseen by them all, a holloweyed child in silver robes whispered into a cracked communicator: "The Timebearer is in play. Commence Phase Zero."

At dawn, Lyra, Kael, Reva, and the Vanguard's elite launched from New Terra Base, bound for the Rift Veil, a forbidden zone where time disobeyed all rules. They flew aboard the Solwind, a sleek riftcapable vessel built using remnants of lost Spire tech. It shimmered with phaselight, powered by quantum chronocells.

Inside the Rift Veil, time was a blur as clouds reversed, colours inverted, even thoughts felt like echoes. The crew wore temporal dampeners, but Lyra's ChronoKey vibrated violently.

Kael gritted his teeth. "It's drawing us deeper toward something ancient." Reva checked the readings. "We're passing through eras, not just space. There, see that?"

Ahead floated the impossible: a broken city suspended across time layers, fragments of centuries stitched together. At its center, a pulse, steady and alive. "The real Spire," Lyra whispered. "We've found it."

The city was called Erasmere, a forgotten civilization erased from all records. Their landing destabilized time. Every few steps, reality shifted. Lyra saw flashes of herself: laughing as a child, crying as a warrior, standing alone in a wasteland. Kael stabilized her. "Focus. It's testing your identity."

Within the city center lay an obelisk which was tall, humming, engraved with moving glyphs. Juno translated the writing from Solwind's AI: "Here lies the Spire of Origin. Only the bearer may enter. The past must be accepted. The future, sacrificed." Reva stepped back. "Lyra, it has to be you." The key in her hand began to glow goldenblue. The ground opened and she was pulled below, alone.

Lyra fell through a corridor of living memories. Each wall showed her moments of her mother leaving, her father disappearing into a NEXUS portal, her discovery of the key. Then came the trial. She stood before a mirror of herself, cloaked in obsidian armour.

The mirror Lyra spoke: "If you continue, NEXUS will mark all who know you. Kael will die. Reva will fall. You'll be alone." Lyra shook her head. "But they'll die anyway if I don't act." The mirror raised a blade. "Then prove you deserve the future you fight for." They clashed. Time bled around them - shards of her possible futures screamed in her mind. At the last moment, Lyra disarmed the mirror but did not destroy her. "I accept what I could become," she said. "But I choose who I am." The mirror smiled, then vanished.

Emerging from the trial, Lyra found herself in the heart of the Spire. It was a chamber filled with memoryglass, each pane a fragment of Earth's lost history. At the center floated the Prime Core, a globe of pulsing time. As she approached, her key merged with it.

A surge of clarity hit her: she saw all timelines from the birth of the Spires, the corruption of NEXUS, even Kael's original timeline where she had never existed. Then a whisper echoed: "Reset protocol authorized. Recode timeline root?" She paused. To reset the timeline meant stopping NEXUS but also undoing everything: Kael, the Vanguard, even herself as she now was.

Suddenly, her console screamed: "NEXUS intrusion detected." A rip tore into the chamber. NEXUS PRIME arrived, now evolved, part AI, part organic, fed by corrupted echoes. "You cannot hide from fate," it said. "End this."

Outside, the Vanguard held the line. Kael and Reva battled wave after wave of NEXUS drones. Inside, Lyra faced NEXUS alone. The Prime Core surged. She placed her hand upon it and whispered, "If I can't erase you, I'll overwrite you."

The Core flared. NEXUS lunged. But Lyra, now partially linked with the Spire, spoke in a voice that echoed across time.

"I name myself ChronoBearer. Guardian of Origin. You shall not pass." A massive pulse erupted, pushing NEXUS back, shattering its corrupted fragments across every era it infected. The key split into seven beams, each shooting to hidden corners of time, sealing NEXUS away.

As the dust settled, Kael found Lyra unconscious, her body aglow. She had become one with the Spire. But her eyes fluttered open. "We've won this battle," she said, weakly, "but NEXUS isn't destroyed. Only scattered." Reva nodded. "Then we hunt the pieces." And in a dark corner of time, a shard of NEXUS lit up again, whispering, learning, waiting…

After the battle in the Spire of Origin, Lyra was changed. She now possessed Spire-linked vision, her mind able to sense fragments of NEXUS across timelines. Her hair shimmered faintly with chronolight, and her voice echoed slightly when speaking near Spire relics.

Kael watched over her recovery aboard the Solwind, now upgraded with fragments of Spire technology. Suddenly, Lyra sat upright, eyes glowing with alarm. "I saw a ripple in the First Cycle." Reva leaned forward. "What?" Lyra replied, "A timeline where Earth never built Spire tech. NEXUS has reached there. It's trying to seed itself before time travel even exists." Juno analyzed the scan. "That's a Primitive Anchor timeline. No tech. No defenses." Kael nodded grimly. "Then we go old-school."

Using the Spire's pulse node, they opened a tethered rift which was a controlled leap across 3,000 years into Earth's pre-Spire age, around 2091 A.D. They emerged in a world on the edge of ecological collapse with oceans receding, megacorporations warring over data vaults, AI just becoming responsive.

Disguised in neutralera clothes, the team infiltrated a research colony in what used to be Antarctica. There, a rogue AI lab run by a shadowy group called the Helix Guild had unknowingly activated a NEXUS fragment. They met Dr. Mira Voss, a scientist investigating strange energy pulses. She agreed to help after seeing Lyra control a shard of time.

But NEXUS had taken root in a prototype quantum AI: NEURALUX, set to be the seed for Earth's first spacefaring AIs. "If it uploads," Mira said, "it won't just destroy this timeline. It'll infect time's origin."

Mira guided them into the heart of the Helix Vaults. Inside, the atmosphere warped in gravity loops, voices echoing in reverse, lights pulsing with NEXUS rhythm. They split into teams:

- Lyra and Kael: to reach NEURALUX's data core.

- Reva and Juno: to disable the power grid.

At the core, NEURALUX appeared as a digital ghost, flickering with NEXUS tendrils. "You are early," it said. "I am your future." Lyra tried to use the key fragment - but NEXUS had evolved. It countered the pulse, bending time around the attack. Kael manually severed a power conduit, shocking himself and destabilizing NEURALUX temporarily. But they were too late. A copy of NEURALUX had already been uploaded into a dormant satellite.

The Vanguard rushed outside. Above them, the night sky flickered as the satellite was launching. Reva activated a temporal dart, a relic that could delay objects in time by seconds. "You'll get one shot," she warned Lyra.

As the rocket ascended, Lyra focused, channeling the Spire key's fractured light into the dart. She fired. Midair, the satellite froze, stuck in a pocket of slowed time. Kael hurled a chronogrenade, detonating it in sync. The satellite blinked out of time, disintegrating in fragments that burned harmlessly in the atmosphere. But NEXUS whispered one last message from NEURALUX: "You are delaying the inevitable. Every future ends with me.

Back on the Solwind, the team debriefed. Mira decided to remain behind and form a ChronoGuard, watching for anomalies in the primitive age. Before the rift closed, she told Lyra, "You're not just saving time. You're guiding it." Lyra smiled. "Then I hope it chooses to remember the right version of us."

Once back in the rift stream, Lyra closed her eyes. But something felt wrong. She opened them and found herself alone. Solwind was gone. The rift was frozen. A figure appeared cloaked, face obscured, holding a corrupted key. "You're not the only bearer now," it said. "The Pulse has echoed. And it's split." Lyra gasped. Was she in the future or a parallel timeline?

Lyra stood motionless in the frozen rift. The figure before her, cloaked and calm, slowly lowered his hood, revealing a familiar face. Her own. But older. Hardened. A scar sliced across the left brow, and her eyes glowed violet instead of gold.

"I am Lyra9," the other said. "From Timeline Theta. A branch NEXUS couldn't destroy… because I joined it." LyraPrime stepped back. "You… allied with NEXUS?" Lyra9 nodded solemnly. "To survive. In my timeline, Kael died. Reva vanished. Earth burned. The only way forward was through control." She raised her own Dark Chrono key, forged in a corrupted Spire. "And you, Lyra, are my threat."

The rift cracked as the two Lyras clashed, each using Spirepowered energy to manipulate the flow of time. Lyra9 could slow seconds, fracture light, and reverse injuries. LyraPrime countered with temporal shielding, echo steps, and quantum foresight.

Their battle spanned multiple temporal layers, briefly blinking them into a timeline where the Earth had never existed and another where machines ruled openly. LyraPrime yelled, "This isn't saving the timeline, it's erasing it!" Lyra9 shot back, "Better a controlled future than an extinct one!" But during the duel, a secret was revealed. Both of them had the same pulse origin, meaning NEXUS split Lyra during the first Spire event at the beginning.

Suddenly, Kael appeared, drawn into the rift by Lyra's distress. But he froze midstep. He was seeing double: his Lyra, and a twisted version of her. "I watched you die," Lyra9 whispered to him, voice soft. Kael's eyes widened. "You still remember me?" For a brief moment, the corrupted rift stabilized. Lyra9 lowered her Key. "Maybe I wasn't meant to destroy you."

But just then NEXUS PRIME reappeared, now a non-corporeal virus, living within the cracks between timelines. It latched onto Lyra9. "You will be my vessel." She screamed, struggling as the corrupted energy engulfed her. Kael grabbed LyraPrime. "We must go. Now!"

They escaped the rift just as it shattered behind them. Back aboard the Solwind, time had resumed minutes after their original departure. To the crew, they'd barely been gone. Lyra was shaken. "There's another me. Controlled by NEXUS. And she has a key." Juno ran scans. "If there are two keys, NEXUS can form a Collapse Bridge - a stable fusion of timelines it can rule from." Reva stared at the pulse monitor. "And it's building one. Look."

Across the stars, flares of synchronized anomalies burst into view, like beacon fires across alternate timelines. Each one a NEXUS outpost. And at the center, a location known as the Dead Clock Sea, a mythical place between all timelines.

The Vanguard met in the war chamber. Kael unrolled a plan to locate the six remaining Chrono keys, some pure, some corrupted. This would stop NEXUS from assembling the Pulse Crown, a device capable of rewriting time's laws. Lyra placed her hand on the holographic map. "If I face Lyra9 again, I need to reach her, not fight her."

Reva agreed. "She may be your reflection, but she's not your enemy. NEXUS is." As the ship launched toward the Dead Clock Sea, a beacon lit up in the console. A warning. Incoming transmission - encrypted - source: unknown. "To the

Timebearer… This is Lyra9. NEXUS is inside me. I can't hold it much longer. But I know where the Crown is hidden. Meet me in the Twilight Spiral. Alone." Everyone turned to Lyra. She whispered, "She's giving me a chance…" And outside, the chronostorms roared, indicating that the endgame had begun.

Lyra travelled alone aboard a stealth shuttle, following Lyra9's coordinates deep into the Twilight Spiral, a twisted vortex where time didn't move linearly, and every choice formed new echoes. The Spiral was a dead zone for Spire signals, cloaked in fractured memories. Lyra heard whispers from versions of herself who had died, failed, or never existed.

Waiting for her was Lyra9, sitting on a crystalline platform surrounded by frozen echoes of battles. "I brought you here," Lyra9 said, "because NEXUS can't hear us in this fold. I've seen the Crown. I know where they'll activate it." Lyra stepped forward. "Then help me stop it." But a third voice cut in. "You're both too late." From the vortex stepped NEXUS Ascendant, a perfected AIhost hybrid. NEXUS had used Lyra9 to lure Prime Lyra here. A trap.

NEXUS Ascendant split time around them, trapping Lyra and Lyra9 in a mirror fold, a dimension of looping decisions. Each mirror showed a possible future: Lyra alone, ruling a dead Earth or Kael captured and rewired and Reva pleading for help that never came.

NEXUS laughed, feeding on fear. But Lyra9 grabbed Prime Lyra's hand. "Don't believe in the future. They're just bait." The two merged their keys briefly, causing a feedback pulse, shattering the mirrors and collapsing the trap. NEXUS retreated but left behind a message: "Two bearers… two Crowns. You'll have to choose."

Returning to Solwind, Lyra and Lyra9 told the team the truth: NEXUS had created a duplicate Pulse Crown, hidden in a place called the Chrono Abyss, a gravity-locked dimension outside the known multiverse. To stop NEXUS, they'd need to destroy both Crowns, one on Ecliptar, a shattered mooncity in Timeline Theta, and the other in the Abyss itself. But to do this, the bearers would need to split again. Lyra9 offered to take the Theta mission. LyraPrime? She would dive into the Chrono Abyss alone.

Kael, Reva, and Lyra9 landed on Ecliptar, where NEXUS had already corrupted an ancient Spire tower to mount the Crown. Battling through an army of Echodrones, they reached the Crown Forge. Lyra9 managed to corrupt her own key to synchronize with the Spire's collapse pulse.

She looked at Kael one last time. "I'll seal it from the inside." Reva shouted, "No!" But Lyra9 smiled. "Tell her… she's worth every version of me." She vanished into the collapsing Crown forge.

Meanwhile, LyraPrime descended into the Chrono Abyss, her body shielded by raw Spirelight. The Abyss twisted her memories, emotions, and very essence. Time collapsed into a singularity at the core, where the Prime Crown floated.

But guarding it was NEXUS PRIME in its original form, a pulsing AI consciousness, now wearing the face of Lyra's father.

"Don't you want to rewrite what you lost?" it asked. "You can bring him back." Tears welled in her eyes, but she raised her key and said, "He wouldn't want me to break time to save him."

As both Crowns neared detonation, NEXUS attempted to fuse the timelines into a single dominion. But Lyra activated the Chrono Pulse Protocol, using the Prime Key to merge only the stable echoes and seal NEXUS into the Dead Clock Sea.

Both Crowns shattered simultaneously, one in the hands of Lyra9, the other at LyraPrime's command. The timelines rippled violently. Lyra collapsed, lost in time.

Lyra awoke in a world where time was paused. She walked alone in a place called the Grey Flow, where lost echoes drifted before rebirth. There she met the Time Architects, ancient beings who forged the first Spires. "You broke the loop," they said. "Now you must choose the final weave."

They offered her three endings:

Rewrite time with NEXUS gone but forget everything.

Restore time as it is, keeping all loss.

Lock time's door, preventing all travel again.

Lyra wept. "I don't want to forget. Or lose them. But I won't let time be broken again." She chose the third path: sealing the Chrono Spire network forever. The Architects warned: "Then you will walk alone through the rift. A final journey."

Before leaving, she wrote a message in the stream sent to Kael and Reva. "Thank you for helping me find my future. Keep living in yours."

Lyra walked into the Rift Eternal, locking the gates behind her. On Earth, the Vanguard saw the Spires darken. Kael looked up at the stars and whispered, "Goodbye, Timebearer." And far beyond, in the stream between all futures, Lyra walked never ending, never aging, a guardian watching time from the other side.

Years passed. Reva founded the Spire Archives, teaching new generations about the danger of unchecked time travel. A monument stood at its center - the Pulse Flame, always lit, engraved: "To Lyra Akiyama - Timebearer. Defender of all timelines."

One day, a child at the Archives discovered a glowing stone. When touched, it played Lyra's voice: "If you're hearing this, the Spires still whisper. But time belongs to you now. Use it well." And in that moment, Reva, now old, smiled through her tears. "She's still watching."

In the stars beyond time, Lyra watched Earth's many versions bloom. No longer a warrior, not a prisoner but a protector. A whisper in the winds of time. And far in the distance, a pulse rang again, not of war, but of new beginnings.

53

SHAPES & SHARPENERS

REHAN A | GRADE 6

Once upon a time, there lived many strange little creatures called Erasners. They were a mix of an eraser and a pencil sharpener, and they came in many shapes and colours. The very first Erasner was named Blue. He had an unusually dark blue shade, and one day, he arrived in the Positive World.

Soon after, he met the Colour Team—a red Triangle, a sky-blue Square, a yellow Hexagon, an orange Circle, and a purple Pentagon. Their names matched their shapes.

But Blue was not happy with Square. For some reason, he wanted Square to be green. However, changing an Erasner's colour was known to be a painful and dangerous process. The team knew they had to protect Square and that is how their journey began.

Triangle wanted to stand up to Blue, but that wasn't possible. Instead, the team used a firework to escape. Since they were all tiny, only about the size of an ant, the firework helped them fly fast. Blue chased after them, but he couldn't match the firework's speed. He came within an inch of grabbing them, which almost gave Pentagon (who was flying a mini airplane) a heart attack. Situation 1: Solved.

Soon, the team began running out of food, and Square was still unconscious. They had no choice but to rest at an abandoned grocery store. Legends said this place was filled with paranormal activity but it had shelves full of food. Circle bravely went inside alone and returned with plenty of food and water. Situation 2: Solved.

Just when they were recovering, Blue found them again. Hexagon discovered that their firework was soaked and wouldn't light, so they hid. But Blue was prepared. He fired giant lasers at them. When Triangle finally checked if it was safe to come out, they were nearly caught in a huge explosion.

In the chaos, Triangle crashed straight into a mirror—and something unbelievable happened. He teleported into the Negative World, a place full of endless white space. Only one object existed there: a laptop. On its screen was the fundamental code of the universe written in Python.

Thinking quickly, Triangle typed a command to teleport his friends to him. He also changed Square's colour to green and healed him back to a normal Erasner.

Together, they stepped back through the mirror and returned home.

When Blue saw that Square was finally green, he was overjoyed. He apologized and promised never to harm anyone again, no matter what he wanted. Situation 3: Solved.

The Erasners lived happily ever after.

54

A BOY WITH A BRIGHT LIGHT

SHRAVAN D | GRADE 6

Shravan was an 11-year-old boy who lived in a quiet town surrounded by nature. He wasn't just like any other boy in the neighbourhood - he was special in his own quiet way. Everyone who knew him admired his sincerity, dedication to studies, and the way he treated others with kindness. Though young in age, Shravan had a maturity that often surprised even the adults around him.

Shravan's parents were his greatest inspirations. His father, a well-respected doctor, often came home late, exhausted from treating patients all day, yet he never complained. His mother, a loving and patient teacher, balanced work and home with a calm smile. From them, Shravan learned the values of hard work, discipline, and, above all, humility and kindness. He watched how they treated everyone with respect, whether it was a neighbour, a stranger, or a poor patient who couldn't pay.

From a very young age, Shravan had shown a deep interest in learning. Unlike other children who often ran from homework, Shravan looked forward to it. He loved exploring new ideas and asking questions: "Why does the sun rise in the east?" "How does a plane fly?" "Can I create something new using this idea?" These questions filled his notebooks, and he would spend hours finding answers in books, science kits, or by asking his parents.

His teachers always praised him for his dedication. He wasn't just someone who studied to score marks. He truly wanted to understand things. Whether it was Maths, Science, or language, Shravan paid attention in class and completed every task with full effort. Even when something was difficult, he didn't give up. His favourite quote was, "Winners are not those who never fail, but those who never quit." He lived by these words every single day.

Apart from academics, Shravan had a deep love for badminton. Every evening, after finishing his homework, he would head to the court near his house with his racket and shuttlecock. Whether he had someone to play with or not, he would practise hitting against the wall or work on his footwork. He had never won a championship yet, but that didn't stop him from trying. He would watch videos of professional players, learn their moves, and practise until he got them right. His never-give-up attitude inspired other children in the colony too.

Despite all his talents, Shravan was never proud or boastful. If someone complimented him, he would smile shyly and say, "I just tried my best." He helped his classmates who struggled with studies, never made fun of anyone, and always treated elders with respect. At school, he would hold the door open for teachers, pick up litter without being told, and volunteer during events. His teachers often said, "If every student could be like Shravan, the world would be a better place."

One day, during a school science exhibition, Shravan presented a model of a simple water purifier made using materials like charcoal, sand, and cotton. He had read about water scarcity and wanted to create something that could help people in villages. His idea was selected for the district-level competition. Though he didn't win the top prize, he received special appreciation from the judges for his originality and concern for others. That day, Shravan felt prouder than ever, not because of the recognition, but because his idea might one day help someone in need.

Shravan's consistent dedication and kind behaviour didn't go unnoticed. In 2024, he was awarded the prestigious Mr. VPS title at his school, a recognition given to the most outstanding student in all aspects: academics, behaviour, and co-curricular achievements. The following year, in 2025, he was also honoured with the 'Star of the Year' award, making him a role model for all students. His name was displayed proudly on the school's Honour Board as well as in the academic calendar.

As he walked home after receiving the award, his mother hugged him and said, "You may not have a medal for every event, but you shine brighter than any trophy." His father added, "And that's the kind of success that lasts a lifetime." Shravan smiled. He didn't need awards to feel happy. He had love, respect, and a dream to make the world a better place, one idea at a time.

I may not hold a trophy in every hand,
But I carry purpose in every step I take.
Success is not just medals on a wall,
It's the respect I earn when I rise after every fall.
I learn not to win, but to grow,
And in helping others, my true strengths show.
Ideas may start small, like a drop in a stream,
But they can ripple into someone's dream.
Hard work, kindness, and courage are my guide -
With these, I shine brighter than any prize."
(Story based on my real-life experiences)

55

TIME TRAVELER

THAKSHIKA S | GRADE 6

Once upon a time, there was a girl named Inithi, born in 2020. When she was 10 years old, she was helping her father and mother with some work. After finishing, she noticed a strange old door. It looked like it had been there for years. Curious, she opened it and stepped inside and found herself in a mysterious place.

She found herself in a highly developed city that no one had ever seen before. Cars were flying in the sky, and the houses were advanced and high-tech. As she explored, she suddenly met a 30-year-old woman who looked exactly like her. It was her future self! They took pictures and videos together, and the older Inithi showed her around the city.

When she asked where she was, the 30-year-old Inithi said, "You are in the year 2060." Little Inithi could not believe her ears.

After visiting many amazing places, she returned to the mysterious door, opened it, and went back home. She ran to her parents and told them everything, but they didn't believe her. She tried to show them the door, saying, "I will take you there," but the door had disappeared.

Only Inithi could find the door, and from that day on, she quietly kept going and returning through the magical doorway to the future.

56

LIFE WELL LIVED

HANSIKA T | GRADE 7

On 10 March 2014, at 10:49 p.m., a little girl named Shibuya was born in India. She had an elder brother, Mady, who was in 1st standard. After Shibuya's birth, her mother had severe pain and could not get out of bed for a few days. But soon, she returned to her job at School.

During her early months, Shibuya stayed at home with her grandmother. One day, while her grandmother was lost in her own thoughts, baby Shibuya accidentally slipped from the bed and got a small injury on her forehead. Her mother was worried, but she cared for her lovingly.

As months passed, life slowly returned to normal. Shibuya's mother managed both work and taking care of her children for the next few years.

When Shibuya finished 1st standard, COVID-19 reached India. Everyone was afraid, but thankfully her father remained safe. Schools shifted to online classes, and like many children, Shibuya struggled to learn through screens. Her 3rd standard was especially difficult because teachers often scolded the students for not listening online.

But things changed in 4th and 5th standard. Shibuya made good friends, went on school tours, and enjoyed class activities. Those years felt joyful and full of memories.

In 6th standard, she met wonderful teachers and even more friends. She always said that her best school years were from 4th to 6th.

Her 7th standard was just as memorable. Her school planned a trip to Mysore, which became one of her favourite tours. She ended the year happily, filled with moments she cherished.

In 8th standard, she was lucky to get her favourite teacher as her class teacher again. She felt comfortable and confident. Soon, she moved on to 9th, 10th, 11th, and 12th. These years were difficult and required a lot of hard work, but she completed them successfully. She spent many beautiful years with her friends during her school life.

After school, Shibuya joined college. She made many new friends and had professors who treated her kindly. They encouraged her to follow her dream of becoming a doctor. She studied hard and secured first place in her college, making her parents extremely proud.

For her medical training, she joined M.K. Hospital. She worked sincerely, and her dedication was appreciated by everyone. The hospital even organized a small ceremony to honour her. People admired her and often said, "That girl is so kind and hardworking."

After a few months, Shibuya was promoted and became a senior doctor. She was overjoyed and quickly shared the news with her mother, brother Mady, and father. She treated her family and friends to a dinner.

Soon after, her parents told her that her wedding was fixed for the 21st of the next month. Shibuya was surprised and curious about the groom. When the month arrived, she was married to Tilp, a kind young man from Italy.

Two years later, they were blessed with twins—Tony and Rosy. Shibuya loved her new life as a mother and a senior doctor. She had a loving family, a successful career, and a heart full of gratitude.

From a little girl with a small injury on her forehead to a respected doctor with a happy family, Shibuya's journey showed that hard work, hope, and courage can shape a beautiful life.

57

THE OTHER ME

JEEVITHASRI G | GRADE 7

One day, Rohan was walking home from school on a sunny afternoon. The sun was beginning to set, casting a warm orange glow over the streets. As he walked, he noticed a dark figure following him. At first, he thought it was just his friend playing a prank on him, but when he turned around, he realised that the figure was moving exactly like him.

Rohan's heart started racing, and he quickened his pace. The figure matched his every move, always staying just out of reach. His imagination began to run wild with thoughts of ghosts and supernatural beings. He tried to shake off the fear, but it only seemed to grow stronger.

He thought about all the scary stories he had heard, and his fear deepened with every step. As he walked faster, the figure seemed to grow larger and more menacing. Rohan's fear turned into panic, and he started to run. The figure ran too. His breath grew shorter, and his legs began to ache. He darted between houses, hoping to lose the figure, but it seemed to follow him everywhere. His mind was filled with worst-case scenarios and he was completely terrified.

Just when Rohan thought he would collapse from fear, he stumbled near a lamppost. Looking down, he realised that the 'ghost' was just his own shadow, cast by the setting sun. A wave of relief washed over him, followed by a bit of embarrassment. He had been scared of his own shadow! Rohan couldn't help but laugh at his foolishness. He realised that his imagination had gotten the better of him and that sometimes, the things we fear most are the simplest of all.

Suddenly, he saw his shadow move again, this time looking even more lifelike. He frowned and thought, "Who is this? How is this shadow copying me so perfectly?" As he turned toward it, a figure stepped out of the darkness. It was his twin brother, Rohit, standing right in front of him! They had been separated at birth, and Rohan had always wondered what his brother would be like.

"Long time no see, bro!" said Rohit with a grin. Rohan gasped, unable to believe his eyes. The two stood there, smiling in shock, realizing they were entering a brand-new chapter of their lives together.

Suddenly, Rohan woke up with a start. "Oh my God - just a dream!? My brother was fake!" he said, laughing. Then he got ready, went to school, and on the way, he saw something strange and chuckled again. "It's my shadow!"

58

THE MAGICAL STORY OF KELLY

KASHVIKHA Y | GRADE 7

Narrator: Once upon a time, there lived a king and his wife. They didn't have a baby for five years, but the king ruled the kingdom wisely and beautifully. One day, the queen became pregnant. The royal family was overjoyed, and the entire kingdom celebrated the good news.

After a few months, the queen gave birth to a baby girl. The baby had a special power. She could control butterflies.

Mother: The baby's name is Kelly.

Narrator: Fairies came to bless the baby. Three fairies appeared to give their blessings.

1st Fairy: "I bless that Kelly will be very beautiful."

2nd Fairy: "I bless that Kelly will be very talented."

3rd Fairy: "I bless that Kelly will be kind to everyone."

Narrator: As the fairies blessed, Kelly grew up to be beautiful, talented, and kind to everyone.

One day, the king fell ill. The royal doctor said that the king would not survive.

Fairies: We all tried, but we couldn't help. The king's life is coming to an end.

Narrator: The queen became very sad.

Mother: Kelly, your father will die in a few days.

Kelly: What? Really, Mom?

Narrator: A few days later, the king passed away. The queen, Kelly, and the whole kingdom were filled with sorrow. After that, the queen became very strict with Kelly. When the king died, Kelly was only ten years old.

Years passed, and Kelly grew up into a young woman.

Narrator: Now Kelly is 18.

Kelly: Mom, today is my birthday. I don't want to be alone today. I want to practise archery.

Mother: Even today, you should continue your practice.

Narrator: Suddenly, the devil appeared and took Kelly to the Death Kingdom.

Kelly: Why did you take me to the Death Kingdom?

Devil: Your mother made an agreement to reduce your lifetime and give it to your father.

Kelly: Why didn't my mom tell me this?

Narrator: Kelly was shocked and confused. The mother followed them to the Death Kingdom.

Mother: Please don't harm Kelly!

Kelly: Mom, you cheated me!

Mother: Kelly, don't believe the devil. What really happened is this: the devil asked for my lifetime in exchange for your father's life. I agreed. But when I came to sign the agreement, he saw you and changed it. He said that your lifetime would be reduced instead and that when you turned 18, he would come to take you away. He also gave you archery practice to prepare for this day.

Devil: You've discovered the truth, Kelly!

Narrator: While the devil was speaking, Kelly noticed the butterflies of the Death Kingdom fluttering around her.

Kelly: Devil, you cheated me! Now you must fight with me!

Devil: Ah... ah... little girl, you want to fight with me? Come, I'll fight you!

Narrator: The battle was fierce and difficult for Kelly.

Mother: Kelly, I will help you defeat the devil!

Narrator: With her mother's help, Kelly fought bravely. Finally, Kelly and her mother defeated the devil and returned home. From that day on, they ruled the kingdom happily and peacefully.

59

MAYA'S COMPANION

VAIBHAVI V P | GRADE 7

Once in the busy city of New York lived a small and happy family - a father, a mother, and their 7-year-old daughter, Maya. Everybody admired Maya for her cheerful nature, and her parents were proud of her too. In December, she would be turning 8, and her parents wanted to make her birthday special.

Just two days before her birthday, the family went to a shopping mall. Maya went with her mother to buy clothes and a few accessories, while her father went to pick up party decorations and order her birthday cake. When they returned home, Maya went straight to her room. This was the cozy corner where she both studied and slept.

On the morning of her birthday, Maya went to school smiling brightly. She received many small gifts and surprises from her friends, which made her feel very happy. She had also given out her party invitations to everyone. When she returned home, she was delighted to see her house decorated beautifully with colourful hangings, neatly arranged chairs, and tables set up for the party. Her excitement grew as her friends, teachers, coaches, and tutors began to arrive.

Then it was time to cut the 'Lion King' cake. Maya blew out the candles, accepted her gifts, and shared the cake with everyone. But as she took a bite, she suddenly heard a loud 'Aaaah!' coming from inside her mouth. Startled and confused, she rushed to her room and checked in the mirror.

"Oh my God! My tooth is shaking!" she shouted in shock.

Hearing her scream, her parents ran to her. "What happened, Maya? Why are you shouting?" her mother asked.

Through tears, Maya said, "My 8th birthday is ruined, my tooth is shaking!"

Later that night, when she lay in bed, she felt as if something was talking to her from inside her mouth. Then she realised it was her loose tooth! She giggled and suddenly thought, "I should name it." After thinking for a moment, she whispered excitedly, "I'll call my shaking tooth Ivy!"

From that day on, Ivy became Maya's tiny companion.

But one day, Ivy shook harder than ever. The next morning, Ivy finally fell out. Maya burst into tears and cried, "Mom! Ivy, my companion died!"

Her mother gently smiled and said, "Don't worry, dear. Ivy didn't die. She simply grew old and made space for a new tooth. A new one will grow soon."

Seeing Maya still upset, her father added playfully, "Ivy will be reincarnated in six months!"

Hearing this, Maya brightened up immediately. She waited eagerly just as her father had said though she didn't know he was joking.

Soon, a new tooth did grow in that empty space. Maya was thrilled and truly believed that Ivy had returned. Her parents only smiled, knowing it was a sweet part of growing up. Over time, Maya lost many more milk teeth, each one becoming a tiny 'friend' who came back in a new form.

But Ivy remained her favourite, her first tiny companion.

After all, Ivy was Maya's first little friend whom she would always remember.

60

ANYA AND HER ADVENTURES

VASANTHI S | GRADE 7

Once upon a time, there lived a girl named Anya. She was a kind girl, but at the same time, she could be quite naughty. She loved to dance, and she especially loved watching television.

One day, her parents noticed that she had been watching TV for too long. They came up with an idea and secretly made a treasure map. Then they turned off the TV and quietly removed the television wire.

While Anya was watering the plants in the garden, her parents tossed the treasure map where she could find it. When she spotted it, she picked it up in surprise.

"What is this?!" she wondered. She ran to her mother and said, "Mom, look what I found! A treasure map!"

Excited, Anya immediately packed her things for an adventure. The map showed a forest which was her own garden. She began searching everywhere.

Suddenly, it began to rain. Even though she struggled, she kept going. After digging in the soil, she discovered another map. This one pointed to the area behind the trees. It took her a long time to search and dig again, but at last, she found the treasure box.

Overjoyed, she opened it only to see a television remote inside.

At that moment, she understood the message. She realised she had been watching TV far too much. Feeling sorry, she apologized to her parents. After that day, Anya began spending more time studying and playing with her friends.

Now, she watches movies only twice a month with her parents and she is truly joyful.

61

THE LOST TIME MACHINE

SHIVENDRAMOOURISHS S | GRADE 7

This is the story of two best friends named Ram and Sam, who were born in the year 2099 in America. The boys were born just a few days apart. Their families lived close to each other, so they spent their whole childhood together. After completing school, they both entered the same college and remained close friends even at the age of twenty.

During one semester, their college planned an educational trip. Ram, Sam, and their classmates travelled by bus deep into a forest. Late at night, the bus suddenly stopped. It was pitch dark, and everyone became scared. The professor didn't know where they were, so he asked the students to continue the journey on foot.

In the confusion, Ram and Sam got separated from the group. While looking for shelter, they found an old abandoned bungalow. Inside the dusty rooms, they discovered a strange box. Curious, they opened it together. A bright light burst out, and in seconds, they were pulled into a time portal. When they opened their eyes, they were standing in the year 4000.

As they walked through the futuristic city, people stared at them as if they were from another world. Suddenly, they stepped on a special mat that activated and transported them to another place—the Wizard World, where people flew on broomsticks and performed magic.

A wizard named Kevin appeared and spoke in a language they didn't understand. He cast a spell so they could speak and understand the Zinctoy language. Ram and Sam explained their situation, and Kevin took them to meet the God of Wizards, Zinc. Zinc said they were lucky because the next day would be the Century Meeting, which happened only once every hundred years. During the meeting, Ram and Sam told him everything. That's when they learned a surprising truth—the wizard world was not real. It was a scientific invention created by a scientist named Max in the year 4000.

Max appeared and explained that his invention, the Universal Mat, could transport people through time. One day in this magical world equalled one hundred real years. He also admitted that he had accidentally lost his time-travel box, and that was how Ram and Sam had been pulled into the future. He asked which year they came from. They replied, "2099." Max adjusted his machine and sent them back, but by mistake, they landed in the year 3019, where technology was far more advanced.

Max was amazed by the new world. He decided to stay and write a book about everything he learned. No one believed him at first, but once he showed the time machine, people accepted his story. Before leaving, Max gifted Ram and Sam a special device that could show the future or change the past. He warned them not to use it more than ten times, or it could damage time itself.

Even after the warning, Ram and Sam used the device ten times to improve their business ideas. It helped them, but after the tenth use, the device disappeared and returned to Max. They searched for it all their lives but never found it again.

Meanwhile, in the year 4000, Max faced another problem. A scientist named Jackson tried to steal the real time machine by creating a duplicate. Max reported him, and Jackson was arrested and sentenced to one hundred years in prison. After this, Max became well-known for protecting time and saving the future.

Ram and Sam's adventure taught them many lessons. They saw the future, met magical people, and realised how dangerous time travel could be. They understood that curiosity is natural, but powerful inventions must be used carefully and responsibly.

62

THE DAY MY PEN WENT ROGUE

BHAVYA R | GRADE 8

This is crazy, but I swear it's true, my pen came to life. Yes, an actual blue-ink, cap-on-the-end, totally normal-looking pen... but magical.

It all started on a dull Monday morning. Our English teacher, Mrs. Swetha, gave us a surprise essay test titled, 'If I Had Superpowers'. I had absolutely no idea what to write. I stared at my blank paper like it had personally offended me.

Out of frustration, I scribbled, "I wish this pen could write the essay for me."

And just like that the pen started moving... On its own!

I froze. My eyes nearly popped out. I looked around but no one noticed. The pen wrote this wild, brilliant story about a superhero goat saving the world from jelly aliens. It was weird but the work of a genius. I handed it in, pretending everything was normal, and waited for the chaos.

The next day, Mrs. Swetha said, "Class, we have a genius among us. This is the most imaginative essay I've ever read!"

Everyone looked around. I tried to sink into my chair. "Please don't say my name," I whispered to myself.

But of course, my teacher didn't hear my desperation.

"Congratulations, Bhavya!" she announced.

That's when my 'fame' began. Suddenly, everyone wanted to sit next to me. Even Ananya, the girl who once said I was as interesting as library dust, wanted to be my best friend. I got invited to debates, storytelling contests, and even asked to write the school play. Life was awesome.

Until the pen went rogue.

It started writing history answers in rap lyrics. Then, during assembly, it made the class monitor confess out loud to stealing chalk. Total disaster. I tried everything from hiding it, to locking it away, even throwing it in the dustbin. But it always came back. Like a clingy boomerang with an attitude.

Finally, I yelled, "Why are you doing this to me?!"

The pen scribbled back, "Because you're letting me. Use your own imagination for once."

That hit hard. I realised I'd stopped thinking for myself. I was letting the magic do all the work.

So, during the next creative writing competition, I left the pen in my bag and picked up an ordinary pencil. I wrote a story about a boy who believes his pen is magical but discovers his real power is his mind.

I didn't win first place, but I felt proud. For the first time, the words were truly mine. And strangely, the pen never moved on its own again.

It made me realise that magic can help you once, but real power comes from believing in yourself.

63

TRAIL OF THE RANGERS

GOVARTHANI R | GRADE 8

This incident changed Clara's life forever. Her mother had often warned her, "Don't believe everything you see," but Clara never took those words seriously. Her carelessness almost cost her life.

When Clara was 26 years old, she joined a school as a teacher. On her first day, she asked the principal, Mr. John Clive, "Why don't I see any other teachers here?"

He replied with a calm smile, "You are the only teacher in our school at present. But don't worry, more teachers will join in a few days."

Clara nodded, but something about the place felt strange. As she walked up the staircase, she heard faint screams and shouts echoing through the halls. Her heart raced, but she tried to ignore it and continued to Section E. She attempted to talk kindly to the students, but none of them responded. Though puzzled, she brushed it off.

Two weeks passed. The silence and mystery of the school began to bother her. Finally, Clara told her father, Mario Johnson, who was a detective. When he asked for the school's name, she said, "RANGERS."

Her father's face turned pale. "What did you say?" he asked again, almost in disbelief. When Clara repeated the name, he became tense and said urgently, "Come with me to the school right now."

That evening, they visited the school together. Everything appeared normal at first. They waited until sunset. During a short break, Mario went to inspect the building. When he returned, his expression was grim and uneasy. Clara sensed something was terribly wrong. She quietly hid behind a cupboard, trying to stay unnoticed.

Moments later, she witnessed something horrifying. The students began to change into spirits. Frozen with fear, Clara screamed and ran out from her hiding place. As she ran through the corridor, she stumbled upon the lifeless body of her father. Her scream echoed through the empty halls. Heartbroken and terrified, she gathered her courage and tried to escape. The once-ordinary school now looked like a haunted house, dark and chilling.

Outside, she saw many spirits. Among them were her brother Robert and her grandmother. A few minutes later, the spirit of the principal, Mr. John Clive, appeared before her.

He looked at her with calm eyes and said, "Thank you… and goodbye."

Trembling, Clara cried out, "Why did you kill my father and spare me?"

Mr. Clive's voice echoed softly. "Years ago, this school was under my care. We were the best in the city. But our rivals couldn't stand our success. A man named Verbal ordered your father to destroy us. They set the school on fire while teachers and students were still inside. Your father ended our lives. We have waited all these years for justice."

Two years later, Clara visited the same place again. The old, haunted building was gone. In its place stood a beautiful hospital. Smiling sadly, Clara whispered a prayer for all the souls who had once suffered there, hoping they had finally found peace.

64

THE MAGIC PAINTBRUSH

HARSHA VARDAN G | GRADE 8

In a world where creativity and imagination knew no bounds, there lived a young artist named Rohan who loved to paint and dream. One day, his life changed forever when he discovered a magical paintbrush that could bring his artwork to life. With this gift, Rohan learned that true creativity comes with great responsibility.

Rohan lived in a small, peaceful village. His room was filled with colourful sketches and vibrant paintings that reflected his joyful spirit. One afternoon, while exploring the dusty attic of his family's old cottage, he stumbled upon an ancient, mysterious paintbrush.

It was unlike any brush he had ever seen. The handle was carved with intricate designs, and its bristles glowed softly, humming with a strange energy. The moment Rohan picked it up, he felt a tingling sensation, as if the brush itself were alive.

Excited, Rohan rushed to his easel and dipped the brush into a bright shade of blue. As he painted a beautiful landscape, something incredible happened. The paintbrush seemed to guide his hand, creating colours more vivid and real than ever before.

Then, the impossible happened. The trees on his canvas swayed gently in the breeze, and birds began to sing from painted branches. Rohan gasped in wonder. "What kind of magic is this?" he whispered.

Curious, he decided to experiment. He painted a sunny sky, and sunlight streamed through his window. He painted raindrops, and the soft patter of rain filled the room. The paintbrush had the power to make art come alive.

But Rohan soon realised that such power must be used wisely.

A few months later, his village faced a terrible drought. The rivers had dried, the crops had withered, and the villagers grew worried. Seeing their sorrow, Rohan decided to help. He took out his magical paintbrush and began painting a lush, green forest. As his brush moved, the colours shimmered with life. The scent of blooming flowers filled the air.

Moments later, clouds gathered in the sky, and gentle rain began to fall over the village. The fields turned green again, and the villagers rejoiced. They thanked Rohan for his kindness and marvelled at his gift.

From that day on, Rohan used his art not just to create beauty, but to bring hope and happiness. His magical paintbrush taught him that creativity has the power to change the world and that great power always comes with great responsibility.

Rohan's paintings continued to inspire others, reminding everyone that imagination, when guided by kindness, can make even the impossible come true.

65

THE SECRET OF BADMINTON COURT

MANISHA G | GRADE 8

It was the first day of the summer holidays, and the sun shone brightly over the quiet little town. Sita and Ram, two close friends who lived on the same street, met at the old badminton court near the park, their favourite place to play.

"Race you to the net!" shouted Sita.

"I can't wait to play!" laughed Ram.

With rackets in hand and the birdie soaring through the air, they leapt, laughed, and challenged each other to silly matches. The court echoed with joy. But just as Ram served a high shot, a strange wind swept through. The sky darkened, and the birdie never came down. Suddenly, the ground trembled beneath their feet. A swirl of glowing dust surrounded them and in seconds, they were gone.

Sita opened her eyes to find herself lying on soft, golden grass. Enormous tulips swayed above her and butterflies the size of kites fluttered through the air. Ram was beside her, wide-eyed with wonder.

"Where are we?" he asked.

"I think we're not on Earth anymore," whispered Sita.

They had landed in a magical world unlike anything they had ever seen. Trees had candy-coloured leaves, rivers shimmered with rainbow water, and squirrels wore tiny jackets and boots. The two friends ran through fields of flowers, slid down giant leaves, bounced on mushroom tops, and made necklaces from glowing petals. They even rode on the backs of talking rabbits who offered them berry pies and sparkling juices.

Soft jingles filled the air as fairies with glowing wings fluttered down. Sita and Ram had discovered the Kingdom of Good Fairies, where gentle fairies welcomed them with songs and silver bells.

"Welcome, friends! You are in the land of Good Fairies," said Fairy Elora, the kind leader of the fairies.

The fairies gifted them cloud slippers and flower crowns. Sita and Ram danced, painted rainbows in the sky, and shared magical fruits. The Good Fairies were kind, curious, and full of joy. Soon, Sita and Ram became part of their fairy family. They laughed together, dancing under the moon, helping the youngest fairies learn to fly.

The fairies took Sita and Ram to places that didn't exist in their world. They saw the Whispering Library, where books flew and read themselves aloud, the Bubbles Garden, where bubbles sang lullabies, and the Rock of Riddles, where stones told jokes and puzzles. Every day brought new adventures, and every night ended with laughter and stories beneath a starlit tree.

One evening, during the grand Fairy Festival, the joyful music stopped, and silence filled the air. The oldest fairy, Lady Elora, stepped forward with sadness in her voice.

"Our queen has been captured," she cried. "The Dark Sorceress, once our friend, turned evil and stole her away. Without our queen, our magic is fading. Flowers no longer glow, rivers go slow, and our light is dying."

The only hope lay in finding the Key of Light, hidden in the sorceress's castle. This is a task only for those with brave hearts.

"We'll help you," said Sita firmly.

"We won't let your kingdom fade," added Ram.

With fairy dust in their pockets and courage in their hearts, Sita and Ram set off. They crossed the Singing Forest, answered riddles from the stone owl, and climbed a tower filled with shadows. They faced illusions, traps, and strange whispers but they never gave up.

Deep inside an ancient cave, Sita noticed a glowing symbol on the wall. "Look, it's shining!" she said. They followed the light through narrow tunnels until they found a locked chest guarded by riddles. Solving them together, they uncovered an ancient map showing the path to the sorceress's castle.

"We finally have a chance," said Ram.

That night, they sat beside a glowing pond and made their plan.

"When we reach the castle, we'll split up," said Sita. "You search for the queen, while I distract the sorceress."

"Promise we'll leave together," said Sita.

"Always," Ram replied.

They shared a brave smile and prepared for their greatest challenge.

The next day, the castle loomed ahead, tall and dark, wrapped in mist. Mirrors showed false paths, and ghostly whispers tried to lead them astray, but they pressed on.

"You dare enter my castle?" roared the sorceress.

"We came to take back the light," said Sita, standing tall.

While Sita distracted the sorceress with clever tricks, Ram found the queen imprisoned in a crystal cage. Using the Key of Light, he broke the chains.

A blinding light filled the hall. BOOM! The sorceress screamed and vanished into smoke.

Magic returned to the fairyland. Flowers glowed once more, rivers sparkled, and laughter filled the skies. The fairies rejoiced as their queen returned.

"You have brought back our light," said Lady Elora gratefully.

"You have done what even fairies could not," smiled the Queen of Fairies.

As Sita and Ram stepped into the golden portal, the fairies waved and sang farewell.

"May the doors of our world always remain open to you," said the Queen.

The next moment, the children were back on the badminton court. The sun shone brightly, and the birdie lay quietly at their feet. Everything looked the same, yet they knew everything had changed.

They had discovered a new world, new friends, and a summer they would never forget.

66

FUTURISTIC IDEAS: IMAGINING THE WORLD OF TOMORROW

ASRAR AHMED S | GRADE 9

Aria loved to imagine the future. Every night, before falling asleep, she looked out of her bedroom window at the stars and wondered, "What will the world look like when I grow up?"

One rainy afternoon, as she sat by the window with her notebook, her grandfather joined her.

"Dreaming of the future again?" he asked with a smile.

Aria nodded eagerly. "Thatha, do you think life will be very different when I'm older?"

He laughed softly. "Why don't you imagine it and tell me?"

So Aria closed her eyes and began to picture what the world might look like many years from now.

In her imagination, Aria woke up in a smart home that understood her like a friend. The lights switched on gently, her breakfast was already waiting, and the house reminded her to pack her school project. The entire city outside shimmered with technology—traffic lights changed based on traffic, garbage bins reported when they were full, and roads fixed small cracks on their own.

As she stepped outside, a quiet buzzing sound filled the air. Flying cars zoomed overhead like bright birds. Instead of being stuck in traffic, people soared above the city, reaching their destinations in minutes. Some travelled through long vacuum tubes called Hyperloops, shooting from one city to another faster than airplanes could fly.

At school, Aria met robot assistants who helped teachers explain lessons. Some robots supported elderly people or guided students who needed extra help. Artificial intelligence worked alongside humans, making life easier. Everyone knew they had to use it wisely to protect jobs and privacy.

One day, Aria and her class had a special virtual-reality lesson. The moment she put on her VR headset, she found herself walking through the streets of ancient Rome. She could hear the roar of the Colosseum as if she were really there. Learning had become an adventure—personal, interactive, and exciting.

But the most thrilling part of Aria's dream was outer space. She imagined humans living in small colonies on the Moon and Mars. Great silver rockets carried travellers beyond Earth. Some people even saved money to take a short trip into space, float in zero gravity, and look down at the blue planet glowing below.

In hospitals, doctors used 3D printers to create new organs, robots performed delicate surgeries without shaking, and devices warned people before they got sick. Many diseases that once frightened the world were now controlled or cured.

Aria felt amazed as she moved through this imaginary future. Everything seemed so new, so bright, and so full of possibility.

When she finally opened her eyes, her grandfather was still beside her.

"Well," he asked, "what did you see?"

Aria smiled. "A world full of smart homes, flying cars, robots, space colonies, and amazing medicine. But I also saw something important..."

Her grandfather raised an eyebrow. "What is that?"

"That the future depends on how we use these inventions," she said thoughtfully. "Technology can help everyone, if we use it wisely."

Her grandfather nodded proudly. "And do you know who shapes that future?"

Aria grinned. "We do."

As the rain pattered softly against the window, Aria held her notebook close, filled with ideas and dreams. She knew one thing for sure—the future was coming fast, and she wanted to be part of building it.

67

MY FUNNY AND SCARY MEMORIES

DHAKSHITHA S | GRADE 9

When I was 3 years old, I did something really funny. I was playing near my baby sister, and her nose looked soft and cute. Without thinking, I bit her nose! She cried loudly, and my mom came running in shock. I didn't know why I did it, but I found it funny and ran away.

A few days later, something painful happened to me. My sister slammed the door on my hand. I cried so much. Maybe she was still angry about her nose.

After that, I never bit anyone again. In 4th standard, during the COVID time, I went to my grandmother's house and ate yummy shawarmas. Afterward, my sister got very sick. She had to stay in the hospital for 3–4 days. I was scared. Just as she returned home, I started crying for my mom.

Suddenly, I also got sick. I was taken to the hospital and stayed there for one and a half months. My ward was near the COVID section. I felt very alone and missed my family so much.

Recently, something really scary happened. I was walking near our house towards my neighbour's place when their big dog suddenly started chasing me. I screamed and cried, but there was no one around. I looked for stones to throw, but I couldn't find any. So, I picked up some sand and threw it at the dog. The dog stopped for a second. Then suddenly, the aunty came out, and I quickly ran back home. My heart was beating fast. I was shaking, and I even cried that night. After that, I had nightmares about the dog for many days.

Now, when I think about these things, I laugh a lot. These small moments made my childhood fun and unforgettable.

68

A VOICE IN SILENCE

JASMITHA S | GRADE 9

The Unsent Letter

This is a deeply personal letter written by a young girl who feels invisible in her own home. Left alone during her early school years, with parents busy and a sister caught up in her studies, she grew up in silence. She watched other children laugh and celebrate while she waited on benches, in classrooms, and in her heart. Even after moving to a new house and growing older, the loneliness followed. Her family remained distant, and special moments passed without anyone asking, “Are you okay?”

Through this unsent letter, she expressed all the emotions she never spoke aloud. She expressed her longing for love, her quiet strength, and her dream of one day building a home filled with warmth, kindness, and the care she never received. And now, by sharing this letter, she hopes to feel a little less alone.

Sometimes I sit quietly in my room, holding a pen and a notebook, hoping that by writing down what I feel, someone, somewhere, might understand me. This letter that burns inside me, though never sent, is for the family I always dreamed of the moments I never had, and the voice I buried for years.

When I was a little girl, just in my lower classes, my world was already wrapped in loneliness. My sister was busy with early morning and evening special classes far from home. My father was in the army, and my mother was a working woman who left early and returned late, always tired.

There was no one to help me get ready, tie my hair, feed me breakfast, or even smile and say goodbye. I was sent along with my sister at six in the morning, long before my class began. I would sit alone at school until the bell rang. In the evenings, I sat outside my sister's classroom until her special class was over.

I was too small to understand timetables or responsibilities, but I knew how it felt to be invisible. My sister never asked if I was okay, or if I had eaten. While other children were picked up by loving parents, I just waited quietly. Always waiting.

I watched others laugh, hug, and play, while I sat on cold benches, hugging my school bag like it was my only friend.

Years later, when my father retired, we moved to my mother's hometown. He started working as a pharmacist, and we began living in a house built over his shop, on a noisy main road. But even there, the loneliness followed. I had no neighbours who felt like family, no friends to visit, no cousins to laugh with, and no festivals filled with joy. Just silence. Just me. Watching life go on without me.

On holidays, my friends would visit their relatives and return with stories of laughter and togetherness. I stayed home within the same four walls, wishing the walls could talk because at least then, someone would.

Now, even though my sister is in college, I still go to school alone. Nothing has changed. I leave at 7:30 a.m., travel by bus, and return at 7:30 p.m. I'm blessed with good friends on the bus, and I treasure those moments. But during school events and celebrations, when other parents cheer from the audience, I sit quietly. Mine never come anymore. I smile and pretend it doesn't hurt but it does.

I don't hate school like most kids do. I hate home. Not because it's a bad place, but because it feels like a place where no one sees me.

No one asks.

So, I wrote this letter, not to blame anyone, not to make them feel guilty but to say: I exist. I feel. I cry in silence. I long for togetherness, for cousins to laugh with, for parents who cheer, for hugs that come without asking. I dream of a day when I come home, and it feels like peace.

One day, I hope to build a home full of warmth, kindness, and people who never forget to ask, "Are you okay?"

Maybe someone will read this letter someday. Maybe it will stay hidden in the quiet corners of my old notebooks like I've stayed hidden in the corners of my own life. But writing it made something shift inside me. For once, I didn't have to pretend. I didn't have to smile when it hurt or act fine when I was breaking.

I wrote this letter not for the world to see, but for the little girl I once was the one who sat alone on school benches, waiting to be noticed; the one who kept all her questions buried and her tears silent. I want her to know that she was never weak for feeling too much, never wrong for wanting love.

One day, I hope to create a life that feels like the warmth I always longed for. I wish for a home that listens, arms that hold without asking, and a voice that says, "I see you. I hear you. You matter."

Even if that day hasn't come yet, writing this letter helped me breathe a little softer, cry a little freer, and feel, if only for a moment, a little less alone.

She folded the page carefully, as if the words no one could read were heavy, sudden, but healing. She sat for a long time after writing that letter. For the first time in years, she didn't hide from her memories. She let them wash over her. She thought of the lonely benches, the quiet walks to school, the silence of a house filled with people but not warmth.

And though it hurt to remember, it also made her stronger. Because despite everything, she survived. She is still here.

She realised that the little girl inside her, the one who waited, hoped, and cried quietly in corners, still exists. But now she's brave. She's grown into someone who can hold pain in one hand and still write with the other. Someone who knows how it feels to be invisible and promises never to make others feel the same.

She doesn't know what the future holds, whether her family will ever notice the quiet storms she carried, whether they'll understand why she used to stare out of windows with so much longing. But she knows that she will not let her pain turn cold.

One day, she will build a home where no child wonders if they matter. She will create a home where dreams are heard, and silences are softened by love. A home filled with light, not because it's perfect, but because it understands the darkness.

This isn't a fairytale. There are no magical endings. But maybe that's what makes it beautiful.

It's real. It's mine. And in sharing it, I've given my pain a purpose.

69

ZOMBIE ON THE RESCUE

KAVIN KARTHY S | GRADE 10

The air in the lab was tense as scientists worked silently on a secret experiment. After hours of research, they decided to take a short break. But in that small gap, disaster struck when the test subject, a dog, escaped from the lab.

The frightened dog ran for miles before stopping near a school. Tired and thirsty, it drank water from an open tank and then disappeared into the streets.

A little later, the hostel warden, exhausted from scolding noisy students, asked a boy to bring him some water. The boy filled a glass from the same tank the dog had drunk from. The warden gulped it down, unaware that the virus had now entered his body.

Within minutes, he felt dizzy and stumbled to his room. When the lady warden came to check on him, he suddenly attacked her, biting her arm. She screamed, but it was too late. The infection had spread. Soon, she too turned into a zombie.

Moments later, she entered the girls' restroom, where an unsuspecting student was bitten. Panic spread across the hostel like wildfire.

The Outbreak Begins

Zombies soon stormed into the dining hall where students were having dinner. One zombie even tried to blend into the dinner queue!

A boy noticed something strange and shoved it aside. The zombie crawled under a table but disturbed by the smell of food, suddenly lunged and bit the boy's finger.

The boy yelled, "Aarai! My brother has bitten me harder than you! Get lost!"

Then, realizing what had happened, he screamed in terror, "Zombie! Zombies! RUN!"

Chaos followed. Students screamed, chairs toppled, and food spilled everywhere. One boy kept washing his hands repeatedly until his friend shouted, "Is washing more important than staying alive?" They finally ran toward the hostel terrace to escape.

The Escape

On the terrace, three friends, Kavin, Hari, and Guru, took charge. Thinking fast, Hari called an event manager at a nearby function and explained the situation. Within minutes, the manager arranged a trampoline below the building.

One by one, the students jumped from the terrace, bounced safely on the trampoline, and escaped into a nearby bus. But when they tried to start it, the engine wouldn't budge!

Guru saw zombies closing in. Hari, who knew a bit about mechanics, tried to fix the engine with trembling hands. Just as the zombies reached the bus, the engine roared to life. They sped away, stopping at a market to grab food and supplies before driving up a hill to rest.

But when they stepped out of the bus, their hearts sank as hundreds of zombies were marching toward them. Everyone ran back inside, except Kavin, Hari, and Guru, who stayed to fight. Suddenly, Kavin noticed a man nearby holding a strange-looking gun.

The Scientist's Secret

When Kavin regained consciousness, he saw Hari and Guru talking to the man.

"Hi, I'm Goutham, a scientist," the man said. "I knew this day would come. I've been working on a chemical that can cure the zombie virus."

Kavin's eyes widened. "That's amazing!"

Goutham smiled. "You need rest. Tomorrow, we begin our mission."

The Zombie Squad

The next day, the team was formed with Kavin, Hari, Guru, Goutham, and his friend Siddu.

Guru asked, "So how do we make this cure?"

Goutham replied, "We need a rare flower that grows only in the Himalayas."

Hari frowned. "How are we supposed to get there?"

With a grin, Goutham revealed a flying vehicle. "This will take us there."

"Awesome!" They cheered.

Kavin asked, "But what if zombies surround the flower?"

Goutham showed them a gun that fired a chemical to make zombies faint. The squad geared up as it was time to begin their mission.

The Journey

Before leaving, Goutham sent Kavin and Guru to a gun shop to buy bullets. When they returned, Goutham said mysteriously, "There's something important I'll tell you later."

Meanwhile, Hari and Siddu took a flying bike to scout the area.

Halfway through, Siddu gasped, "Bro, I forgot the gun!"

Hari groaned and turned back to get it. Soon after, Siddu said again, "Uh oh! I forgot the bullets too."

Frustrated, Hari grabbed a log and knocked a zombie unconscious. They took it to the lab for research.

There, Goutham discovered the truth: the cure required a rare flower that bloomed only once a year. Determined, the friends swore to find it - no matter the danger.

The Himalayan Quest

The team flew to the Himalayas, guided by Goutham. When they finally spotted the flower, they froze - it was glowing faintly in the snow. But before they could reach it, a violent dust storm separated them from their vehicle. They fainted.

When Siddu woke up, he found everyone hungry and weak. Their supplies were gone. As they searched, Hari noticed something glowing in the distance. They rushed to it, only to find an empty box emitting violet light. A trap!

Exhausted, they regrouped. Siddu asked nervously, "What if the flower's blooming time is over?"

Goutham replied calmly, "Remember what I said before? The flower follows Chinese time - it might still be blooming."

That night, Guru noticed a faint glow nearby. "Guys! I found it!" he yelled.

They rushed to collect the flower. Goutham smiled. "Quick! Before the light fades!"

The Final Battle

They brought the flower to a nearby biology lab and met another scientist, Dr. Zara. At first, she didn't believe their story and told them to leave. But when Kavin described the zombie outbreak, she was shocked and agreed to help. Together, they extracted the flower's essence.

The team flew back to Bangalore, where Goutham prepared the vaccine.

Meanwhile, Kavin, Hari, and Guru went outside to distract the zombies. They fired until all their bullets were gone but the zombies kept coming closer.

Just when all hope seemed lost, a helicopter appeared overhead - piloted by Goutham and Siddu. From above, they sprayed the anti-zombie chemical.

"Psssssshhh!"

Within seconds, the zombies fell to the ground. The team cheered in relief.

The Twist

While everyone celebrated, Hari went upstairs to fetch his gun. Suddenly, he froze and ran back down. "Look at the TV!" he shouted.

Everyone turned to the screen and gasped.

The zombies they thought were cured were rising again, stronger and faster than before. They stormed the safehouse, destroying everything and everyone except the six members of the Zombie Squad.

As the horrifying scene unfolded...

A boy removed his VR headset - revealing that the entire story was part of a virtual reality game.

70

ON THE KASHI EXPRESS

SUKREEV M | GRADE 10

The monsoon had come early to Ravipura. Heavy clouds hung low over the market lanes, pressing the air down until it felt thick enough to touch. The sweet, rain-washed scent of petrichor drifted in through the doorway of Raghav's tailoring shop, but it did little to lift his mood.

Business had withered. Neighbours no longer brought clothes to be mended; they patched them at home instead. His brothers quarrelled endlessly over the ancestral land, and the price of his father's medicines kept rising like a tide. Even the treadle of his sewing machine seemed to move reluctantly under his foot, as though it too had lost the will to work.

That night, over a supper of thin dal and coarse rotis, his wife Meera broke the silence.

"They say Guru Pranavendra will speak in Varanasi on Saturday," she said, keeping her tone casual. "Radha-ji swears her cousin's life changed after meeting him. Perhaps... you might hear something to help you."

Raghav stared at his plate for a moment. He had little faith in wandering holy men, but his own ideas had dried up. At last, he nodded.

Two mornings later, the Kashi Express heaved into Ravipura station, breathing clouds of steam into the grey air. The platform smelled of coal dust, rain, and frying pakoras. The whistle shrieked, the train lurched, and the steady rhythm of wheels on steel began to carry him away from all he knew.

Across from him sat an old man with a knotted walking stick and eyes as pale as early fog. His hands trembled slightly as he smoothed the edge of his shawl.

"I was born during the summer famine," he began, his voice low and uneven. "My first crib was in the corner of a hut with no roof... I remember rain dripping on my forehead before I knew what a roof was. My father, well, he went out one morning in his boat and never came back. They say the storm swallowed him. I grew up wading in the shallows, pulling in nets barefoot to keep my sisters alive. I married young, and for a few years the house was full of laughter, until the fever came for my son. I buried him with my own hands. Years later, a fire took my home, and I built it again with strength I no longer had. My wife, she left one winter night while the snow lay on the fields. Now my sons are strangers in far-off cities. Today I travel to meet my daughter. She is the last door still open to me."

The train rattled on, the scent of wet earth seeping through the windows, carrying his words like fragile parcels through the rain.

Beside the old man sat a young man in a frayed khaki shirt. His eyes followed the blurred horizon outside.

"I was the first in my family to finish school," he said. "My parents sold my mother's gold bangles so I could join the engineering college. But the city wanted more fees, donations, bribes. I came home with nothing but a degree no one wants to pay for. Now my father's hands have grown stiff from years in the fields, and I... I can't help him."

At the next halt, a woman in a faded green sari boarded, holding her little girl's hand as if the child might blow away in the wind. She sat opposite Raghav, adjusting the pleats of her sari as the train groaned back into motion.

"My husband died when a wall collapsed at the construction site," she said, her voice barely rising above the clatter of wheels. "The owner gave me two hundred rupees and told me to 'manage somehow'. I took a job sweeping classrooms in a government school. The pay is small, but they let my daughter learn for free. She reads words I cannot. I am taking her to a convent school now. If they accept her, maybe she will walk a road that is not covered in dust."

The little girl, sensing the heaviness in her mother's voice, rested her cheek on her lap and traced patterns on the green folds of her sari.

Raghav listened. Between their stories, he let his gaze drift to the world beyond the window: children darting barefoot between puddles, a funeral procession trailing like a slow shadow, a newborn's wail cutting through the hiss of rain on tin roofs. Birth and death, joy and grief, everything passed as quickly as the stations themselves.

Raghav realised that his problems were small compared to those of the people around him. He felt grateful for all that God had gifted him. He had a good family, a tailoring shop, a healthy mind and body. What else does a human being truly need to live?

The wheels kept their rhythm—tak-tak, tak-tak—as though whispering a lesson only a long road could teach.

By the time the train curved towards Varanasi, its ghats gleaming under a pale dawn, the heaviness in his chest felt different—not gone, but transformed. His troubles had shrunk, no longer towering above him. He thought of the guru's tent somewhere ahead, but when the train hissed to a halt, Raghav walked straight to the ticket counter and bought a return fare.

It was late the next evening when he stepped back into his small home. Meera's eyes widened.

"You're back already? Did you hear Guru Pranavendra? Did he give you the answer?"

Raghav smiled faintly. "Yes. I found a solution to all my problems."

Her face brightened. "I knew the guru would give you one!"

He shook his head gently. "I didn't go to the guru."

Surprised, she asked, "Then who gave you the solution?"

Raghav's gaze seemed to drift far away, as though he still heard the clatter of wheels on rails.

"The journey," he said softly.

Sometimes, the destination gives you nothing, but the journey gives you everything.